Wild Wings

Part of the WINGS trilogy
Tales of survival, magic and adventure and of
wildlife in all its fascinating and true detail

OTHER TITLES IN THE SERIES
On Silent Wings
Sky Wings

Reviews of the Series:
'Puts Don Conroy's owls on an equal footing with
Richard Adams's rabbits (*Watership Down*) and
Tom McCaughren's foxes'
EVENING HERALD

'a welcome addition to the rank of
Irish novels for children'
CHILDREN'S BOOKS IN IRELAND

DON CONROY

Well known from television for his expertise on wildlife, Don is also an artist, specialising in nature illustration and cartoons, and a storyteller. He has made a particular study of the barn owl. He has written many books.

OTHER BOOKS BY DON CONROY
The Celestial Child

THE WOODLAND FRIENDS SERIES
FOR YOUNG READERS
The Owl Who Couldn't Give a Hoot!
The Tiger Who Was a Roaring Success!
The Hedgehog's Prickly Problem!
The Bat Who Was All in a Flap!

LEARN TO DRAW
Cartoon Fun
Wildlife Fun

FOR ADULTS AND CHILDREN
Bird Life in Ireland
text: Jim Wilson, illustrations: Don Conroy

WILD WINGS

Don Conroy

THE O'BRIEN PRESS

DUBLIN

This revised and re-edited version first published 1995
by The O'Brien Press Ltd.,
20 Victoria Road, Rathgar, Dublin 6, Ireland.
First published 1991.

BRITISH LIBRARY CATALOGUING-IN-PUBLICATION DATA
Conroy, Don
Wild Wings
I. Title
823.914 [J]

ISBN 0-86278-418-2

The O'Brien Press receives assistance from
The Arts Council / An Chomhairle Ealaíon.

2   4   6   8   10   9   7   5   3   1
96 98 00 02 04 03 01 99 97 95

Cover illustration: Don Conroy
Cover design: O'Brien Press Ltd.
Cover separations: Lithoset Ltd., Dublin
Printing: Guernsey Press, Guernsey C.I.

Man's heart away from nature
becomes hard;
lack of respect for growing living things
soon leads to lack of respect
for humans, too.

Sioux Chief Luther Standing Bear

CONTENTS

DEDICATION
To my family and friends

THE NIGHT OF THE WORLD

In heavy waves darkness
Surged through the glorious world
Ravaged it and laid it waste
They saw with horror the destruction
Of all that was beautiful
And they lamented saying
How came this to pass?
For this was not our will
For this was not in our thoughts.

from The Sacred Book of Ravens

CHAPTER 1

Ill Wind in Springtime

A harsh *kee-kee-kee-kee* cry pierced the air as the male kestrel circled above the tree. The distress call signalled approaching danger. Inside the tree trunk the hen kestrel sat brooding new-laid eggs, body tensed as her mate continued to call loudly.

Craning her neck to peer through the narrow hole in the tree the hen kestrel could see no danger. Neither could she see her mate. What could be causing him so much anxiety? she wondered. Rooks mobbing him perhaps? But then he would call in annoyance, and he could always out-manoeuvre them with his swift flight. Was it stoat, mink or rats? Perhaps it was those pesky magpies; they were always bothering her when she was on the wing.

The two of them had searched for several weeks before finding this site, a sheltered resting place in the depths of an old beech tree. Her mate had had to prevent jackdaws from pinching their valuable roost, and he had also fought bravely with hooded crows who were getting too close for comfort.

The hen kestrel sat tight on the new-laid eggs, not wanting them to get chilled. The winds blew cold outside and she remembered how fierce they could be. Only the other evening one of the bigger branches was torn off the leafless tree and fell crashing to the ground. She recalled how frightened she had been and how she had wanted to fly out into the night. Her mate had calmed her down and told her how much more dangerous it would be outside. He had nuzzled gently at the nape of her neck with his bill; it gave her such a sense of security that she had slipped into a gentle sleep, despite the raging storms.

*　　*　　*

Two men were walking across the field towards the tree. The male kestrel sat high up on a nearby elm, and watched the men approaching. They stopped just in front of the tree where the nest was. Rising frantically from his perch the kestrel shot like an arrow over the beech, screaming with all his might.

'He seems upset,' said one of the men, named Matt.

'It's one of those hawks, isn't it?' suggested Mick, his companion.

'Yes,' said Matt, 'It sure makes a racket.'

The hen, hearing the voices, became very agitated. She could sense how close they were.

'You can do the honours, Mick,' said Matt as he started up the chainsaw. 'Remember, it takes skill to use this machine.'

'Are you trying to teach your Granny to suck eggs?' said Mick. 'Just watch how quickly I get this tree down.'

The old tree trembled as the saw tore into its bark. The hen called in alarm, her body shaking from the vibrations. She knew something terrible was happening: the dreadful sound was directly under her. Reluctantly she made her escape, leaving behind her five speckled eggs. Down below, the men were so busy felling the dead tree that they didn't notice the terrified female flying off towards her mate.

'That's it,' said Mick, as the tree fell crashing to the ground.

It was when they began to cut the trunk that Matt noticed the eggs strewn on the clay. 'Look, Mick,' he said, 'there must've been a nest inside this old tree. There're a couple of broken eggs here ...'

'That's why the hawk was so upset,' said Mick. 'Oh, well, too bad. Nothing can be done about it now.'

Matt fingered the cracked eggs gently. 'Still warm!'

'What do you mean,' said Mick, 'I'm blooming freezing.'

'I mean the eggs!' said Matt. Noticing that one of them was still intact, Matt carefully wrapped it in a handkerchief and placed it in his top pocket.

'What's this, a treasure hunt?' enquired his companion.

'No, it's just ... one of the eggs is okay,' Matt replied. 'I might bring it over to that falconer chap who owns the falconry. He might be able to do something with it.'

'Ah, Matt, you have a soft heart, in spite of your gruff ways,' teased Mick.

'Don't start blabbering about it in the local tonight, do you hear me?' warned Matt.

'My lips are sealed,' replied Mick with a snigger.

From a nearby chestnut tree the kestrels watched the destruction of their nest.

*   *   *

The common buzzard roused himself and preened his breast feathers. The tawny eagle called in annoyance, and the cara cara tried to hide behind his perch. More visitors to the falconry! The golden eagle watched the two men walking towards the entrance. The dogs barked loudly.

'Quiet,' shouted a man from inside the house.

Matt knocked on the door marked 'Office'.

'Ah, good morning,' said the falconer.

'Good morning,' said Matt. He introduced himself and his friend.

The falconer greeted them with his right hand. His gloved left hand held a fierce-looking goshawk. Matt and Mick stepped nervously back from the goshawk.

'She won't touch you,' the falconer assured them. 'I've just been imping her up.'

The men looked blank.

'What I mean is, I've been repairing her tail feathers. She somehow managed to break them on her bow perch early this morning. You're a stupid bird, aren't you,' he said, wagging his finger at her, then stroking her gently.

The two visitors gazed in awe at the way the falconer could pet this fierce-looking bird without getting a sharp peck.

'They look perfect,' said Mick. 'You could never tell they'd been broken.'

'It's very difficult at first to do it,' said the falconer, 'but you get the hang of it after a while. Now, gentlemen, what can I do for you?'

'Oh, yes,' said Matt, almost apologetically. He inserted two fingers into his top pocket and removed the check handkerchief carefully, unfolding it like a magician about to perform a trick. The falconer looked on with curiosity while Mick fixed an anxious stare on the goshawk. She glared right back.

'Ah, a kestrel's egg!' exclaimed the falconer.

'That's right,' said Matt. He explained how they had come across it.

'Old trees are useful for hawks and owls to roost in, you know,' the falconer remarked.

He held the egg in his hand. 'It's still warm!'

'Yes,' replied Matt, 'We were wondering if you could do something with it.'

The falconer lifted the egg to his face and pondered for a moment. 'Well, I don't have any female kestrels to brood it, but I could put it in the incubator and see if it would hatch out.'

'That would be great,' said Matt. 'To tell you the truth, I'm feeling a bit guilty about removing that old tree from the field. Well,' he continued, 'we won't take up any more of your time.' He looked over his shoulder at all the other birds, 'I see you have your hands full!' and smiled broadly.

'Thanks for coming. I'll do my best with this little egg,' said the falconer.

CHAPTER 2

Hatching Out a Plot

Surrounded by liquid darkness a tiny creature suddenly became aware of edges to his world. His buckled legs touched solid surfaces. Twisting and hammering with all his might he chipped away at the wall of his dark cave until a small circle of light appeared. He kept on chipping, instinct forcing him on. He was determined to free himself. At last, crawling out from the darkness, all his energy spent, he lay exhausted.

Twenty-eight days had passed and a young kestrel had just been born.

*   *   *

The birds in the falconry sat bolt upright, watching the Nusham. They were used to the Nusham coming to stare, but not at this time of day. The heavy footfalls in the gravel made the birds feel nervous, causing the tawny eagle to call out in annoyance. The Nusham who fed them was there, but he seemed agitated.

The three Nusham walked past the peregrines, who swooped from their perches and lay with wings spread on the grass as if dead. The common buzzard sprang from his perch at them. He flew the length of the cord fastening him to his block. One Nusham recoiled in fright.

The cara cara tried once more to hide behind his perch but the men passed by and stopped at the golden eagle. The eagle didn't budge; he let them come up very close. They stared long and hard at him, then put a hood over his head. They checked him thoroughly: first his feet, then his wings, then his feathers. Finally, removing the hood, they examined his mouth and eyes. After making some notes in a book, the men moved away, talking among themselves. The golden eagle returned to his block, roused himself, then sat hunched.

*　　*　　*

Later, when there was quietness in the falconry, the birds began to talk among themselves.

'It can only mean trouble when Nusham start snooping around like that,' insisted the cara cara.

'It can mean travel,' said the red-tailed hawk. 'You might end up in a dark box for hours, maybe even days. And wake up in some completely new place, watched over by a Nusham you've never laid eyes on before, or beside other birds and animals that resent your presence. It's happened to me twice.'

'They would never do that to the golden eagle. He's

been here longer than anyone else – apart from the black vulture and the griffon,' the red kite declared.

The golden eagle glanced once in their direction, then turned away.

'You shouldn't have mentioned Griff. You know he still gets upset thinking about him,' whispered the peregrine.

But the tactless cara cara blurted out: 'What a way for such a majestic flyer to end it all – in a watery grave ...'

'Are you insinuating that Griff deliberately drowned himself?' the common buzzard snapped. 'Sheila the heron told us how it happened, and I believe her. Griff would have made it to Africa only for the fact that the cord dangling from his leg caught on the trees.'

The cara cara gazed at the common buzzard in disbelief, but said nothing.

'It was in trying to free himself that he fell headlong into the canal,' insisted the common buzzard.

'Griff was in no fit state to fly anywhere, let alone Africa. Those are the facts,' the cara cara said firmly. 'If a swallow can fly to Africa in about six weeks on those little wings, Griff could easily have done it in half the time,' said the black kite, but added, 'he'd need to be in the whole of his health for it.'

'I agree,' said the peregrine.

'So do I,' echoed the red-tailed hawk.

The other birds snapped their bills in agreement.

'Let's face it, Griff was too old to make that flight,' said the cara cara. 'He knew it. But he just didn't want to end up falling off the block and gasping his last breath with one leg tied to a perch.'

'Could we just change the subject?' The severe voice of the bateleur eagle surprised them all. 'Can't you see how much it upsets the golden eagle – and myself for that matter.'

The others nodded, embarrassed. The golden eagle lapsed into silence and did not speak again for weeks. There was an air of despondency.

* * *

Weeks passed. Each day was filled with strange sounds. The young kestrel wondered about the many voices he could hear from his mews. The Nusham was the only living creature he had ever seen. He would leave the young bird small pieces of meat to eat, and sometimes dead day-old chicks. The kestrel preferred the chicks. He liked to pull and tear at them, eating the head first, then polishing off the remainder! After several hours he would cough up a pellet of undigested feathers and bones.

There was a large stone in the mews and the young kestrel used to rub his bill along it – this kept it filed. He wondered what had been here before him. The walls were heavily marked with white and brown splashes and there were some long primary feathers strewn about that he played with when he got bored.

Shafts of sunlight poured in through the wooden laths. He sat most of the time peering out, but he could only see the backs of the other huts. Occasionally, craneflies ventured in through the laths. The kestrel would swoop at them from his branch perch. Most of the time he caught them. They were delicious!

Moths were another welcome addition to his diet. But the bluebottles were a nuisance, as were horse-flies; they would sometimes land on his head and walk across his eye and he never ever managed to catch them. Sometimes he would sidle along the branch and pull a bit of the old bark from it. He enjoyed that a lot. Another favourite thing was to flap his wings furiously while remaining in the same spot. He enjoyed preening his new feathers, as the downy ones were all gone. Some of them had drifted out through the window; others stuck to the branches with the white splashes.

Sometimes he caught a glimpse of birds flying over the treetops. They were different sizes and shapes but they all looked black against the sky. In the evening he would watch the trees melting into the shadows and then he would sleep, only occasionally being wakened by strange hooting or shrieking sounds ...

One day the Nusham came in, carrying something in his hand which wasn't food. He brought it close to the bird's face. The kestrel became very nervous and began to flap his wings.

'Easy now. Just let me slip this hood over your head and I can get down to work.'

Everything went dark. The kestrel felt the man's strong hands as they gripped his body, then laid him on his back. The young bird was terrified. His hearing

became sharper. He could feel the Nusham doing something with his legs. There was a sudden tightness. In the total darkness he wondered would he ever see daylight again.

'There you are, fella,' said the Nusham, removing the hood. 'That wasn't too painful now, was it?'

The kestrel raised himself, bobbed his head and planned to escape out through the window. He leapt off the falconer's glove and flapped furiously, but got nowhere.

'Steady on!' The man lifted the kestrel back on to the glove. The kestrel leapt off it again and ended up hanging upside down. The falconer again placed him on the glove and the kestrel jumped from it once more.

'We could keep this up all day!' The man was still patient though, and simply put the kestrel back on the glove. He picked up a small piece of red meat, waved it in front of the bird's eyes, then rubbed it across his feet. The kestrel grabbed the meat in his claws and looked around, wondering if he could bring it to a high perch. Finally, he relaxed and began to eat the morsel. When it was finished the man produced another small piece. The bird gulped that down too, looking to the falconer for more.

'That's enough for the moment. You're learning fast!' the man said as he carried the bird back to its perch. When he had gone, the kestrel picked furiously at the new jesses on his legs but couldn't remove them. All evening he picked at them. Still they held tightly to his legs. Exhausted, he fell into a deep sleep.

Early next morning a small bird, a blue tit, ventured near the window. It was very colourful, blue cap with yellowish body, face white with black markings. The kestrel sat bolt upright, watching this charming visitor. The bird explored around the frame of the window in search of spiders or other small insects. It moved with great agility, one moment hanging upside down, the next sitting upright.

The blue tit slipped in through the wooden laths, took one look at the kestrel, made a high-pitched *zee* sound and flew out again through the narrow gap. It then flew on into the garden at the back of the falconry. There it would search the apple tree for green caterpillars.

CHAPTER 3

Birds of a Feather

Early one morning, before the Nusham was awake or the dogs were about, the common buzzard watched the cara cara talking with a magpie. They seemed engrossed in conversation for quite a while.

It wasn't long before all the other birds in the falconry became aware of the conversation taking place between the magpie and the cara cara. Some months earlier the cara cara had convinced the magpie to bring him any news that would be of benefit to the falconry, and in return he would give the magpie scraps of discarded meat, or feathers with which to line its nest during the breeding season.

They were all curious to know what the magpie had to relate. But just then the Nusham appeared and the magpie took himself off in quite a hurry, leaving a very shocked-looking cara cara behind.

As he walked around the falconry the Nusham would stop and throw dead day-old chicks to each bird. The sparrowhawks and kestrels got two each.

The bigger birds, like eagles and vultures, would get ten or more. The owls usually got three each, except for the eagle owl and snowy owls, who would get as much as the eagles.

The birds ate their food with gusto, as usual, but there was an air of mystery in the falconry. They were aware that the magpie had brought some terrible news, but no talk could take place until all the Nusham visitors had gone. Every day, Nusham arrived at the falconry, looking at the birds, admiring them, sometimes poking at them. The birds hated this, but today they had other things on their minds.

At last they were on their own again and the goshawk demanded to know what the magpie had told the cara cara. When he had the attention of all the birds the cara cara spoke gravely, 'We are all doomed!' he cried. 'Soon we will be replaced ... no more breeding ... no more nest building ... no more singing to attract a mate ... no more rearing young ...'

'What on earth are you going on about?' demanded the imperial eagle.

The barred owls whispered among themselves that since the cara cara was confined in this place he had no chance of breeding anyway, adding that even if he could escape he was now long past the breeding stage.

As if overhearing the owls' remarks the cara cara continued: 'I'm not speaking about myself or anyone here. I think we all know our fate by now. I'm speaking about the future of birds as we know them.'

The black vulture growled. 'You haven't told us *anything* yet, except make all these wild statements! What do they mean?'

'Do you see that empty mews over there beside the dog kennels?' the cara cara snapped. They all looked towards it, except for the golden eagle who was still picking at his food. 'Have you ever seen a bird being put in there?' The others shook their heads. 'Even a wild one, or an injured one?'

'No, we haven't,' the common buzzard replied, scarcely able to contain his excitement. 'Not for a long time.'

'Quiet!' shouted the imperial eagle, and called on the cara cara to continue.

'There's a bird in there at this very moment,' the cara cara squealed in terror. His tone of voice was disturbed, but his companions couldn't make out why.

'What's all the big fuss about?' the eagle owl asked sharply. 'If there's a bird there, so what? It may have been slipped in by the Nusham ...'

'One of us would have noticed,' a peregrine retorted. 'Day *or* night.'

'The Nusham has discovered how to *make* us!' intoned the cara cara, in a doom-filled voice.

'Wh–what do you mean?' spluttered the red-tailed hawk.

'They have found the secret of our life and can now produce replicas! These replicas look like us, sound like us, fly like us, even eat like us! But they're not really birds as we know birds. They'll simply be slaves for the Nusham!'

'This sounds like nonsense to me,' insisted the snowy owl. 'We've all seen birds forced into sitting on the arm of the Nusham, or flying around the sky for a morsel of food, or singing from a tiny cage like some canaries have to, but ...'

'But the cara cara is saying that this bird has been created by the Nusham to replace us!' the red kite argued.

'And it looks like a kestrel,' said the cara cara.

The two kestrels present became very nervous. 'Are you sure?' they enquired.

'I was told that the Nusham had *created* a kestrel,' said the cara cara. 'The magpie was able to see everything from his home in the ash tree!'

By this stage, there was a general air of shock and absolute amazement among the birds of the falconry.

'How did the Nusham manage it?' enquired the common buzzard.

'Some kind of machine, the magpie reckons,' the cara cara said firmly. 'Today it's a kestrel ... tomorrow it could be an eagle ... or an owl ... or a hawk ...'

'Well, I think we're all working ourselves up into a state because of what some opportunistic magpie has to say,' the black vulture pointed out. 'Let's just keep a close eye on things and if a kestrel comes out from that empty mews, *then* we can begin to worry ...'

The sky darkened and rain began to pour down in torrents.

CHAPTER 4

Winds of Change

Next morning the clouds had dispersed and the falconry was bathed in sunlight. Most of the birds sat with open wings, allowing the warm sun to dry off their feathers. In the empty mews beside the dog kennels, the young kestrel sat by a narrow window, peering out. He could see lots of house sparrows flitting about a laurel bush. A cabbage-white butterfly was bouncing in the air.

Young starlings called from under the eaves of the roof, a hungry brood of five. The dedicated parents would take turns feeding them, flying straight from the fields, carrying leather-jackets or insects. The female would give a small call, and this was followed by the youngs' excited hissing and squealing as they competed for the morsel. Then she would dart away in search of more food, while the male sat anxiously on a telegraph wire ready and waiting to deliver his beakful.

The kestrel heard a footfall along the gravel and

knew it was the Nusham. He felt nervous. He sensed that this day would be a very different day. He didn't know why, but there was an expectation within him. The latch was lifted and the door opened quickly. Dazzling light poured in, making him blink.

'Well, little fella, today you're going to see the big world, join all your feathered companions and start to earn your keep!' The falconer placed a gloved hand at the back of the kestrel's legs, gently rubbing them. The young kestrel stepped back on to the glove. The man laced a leather cord through the small slits in the jesses and wrapped the cord around his two fingers. Then he carried the young kestrel out into the sunlight. The bird trembled in the glare of the day. He jumped off the glove and tried to fly towards the trees, but the cord held him fast.

'Settle down, now.' The falconer placed him again

on the glove and stroked his breast feathers, as he walked towards the circular area where the birds of the falconry were perched.

*   *   *

They were all sitting upright, staring. The young kestrel felt very tense, seeing all the different birds. His eyes searched for a means of escape. The quick flapping of the imperial eagle made him cower. So many birds, most of them much bigger and stronger than he, with a fierce stare in their eyes! A strange sound came from the huts. Later, he was to discover that they housed different species of owls, but for now everything was completely new to him.

The falconer placed him on a perch beside two kestrels and a sparrowhawk. He leapt off the perch but quickly realised that he was tied to a metal ring. He lay on his stomach with wings spread out. The Nusham laughed and went inside.

The soft grass was nice to lie on. He looked up. The sky seemed so vast. The tall trees that surrounded the falconry held high perches which he wished he could reach. None of the birds spoke to him, but he knew they were all watching. He looked over at the cara cara. It just glared back.

The young kestrel spent most of the morning lying spread-eagled. Eventually he sat up, then flew on to his perch. The sun rose high in the clear sky. He felt warm, basking in its light. He preened a little. Greenfinches fluttered overhead.

* * *

In the late afternoon, after he had fed most of the birds, the Nusham stopped beside the young kestrel, who had managed to get himself all tangled up and was hanging upside-down from his perch. The Nusham quickly untangled him and left an extra piece of food for him.

'You'll settle in soon. I think I'll leave you out tonight. It looks like it'll be a mild one.'

The kestrel leapt on to his food, a dead chick, and began to pluck off some of the downy feathers. The other kestrels mantled their food, as if to protect it from this intruder.

After the food was eaten the young kestrel wiped his bill on the grass, picked between his toes at some tiny feathers stuck in his talons, then flew up on to the perch. He looked around him again and observed his new world. Lapwings flew high in an irregular line across the sky. They moved with slow wingbeat. The young kestrel felt the luring call of the sky. He glanced over at the golden eagle, who had been watching him. That great bird now sat, isolated and statuesque, in his hut. He seemed absorbed in himself.

Meanwhile the young kestrel was being discussed by the other birds. 'He certainly could pass for a bird,' said the barred owl.

'Well, we've observed him for most of the day,' said the cara cara. 'As you can see he's a perfect replica of a young falcon!'

They all snapped their beaks in agreement.

'But, my friends, we're not fooled, are we? This creature,' he continued, indicating the young kestrel, 'has been placed here by the Nusham to find out all about us. He's a spy! The plan is to replace us all with his type. He'll watch, observe and mimic us, and who knows, one by one we'll be replaced until we won't know whether we're talking to a real bird or a replica! I say we should have nothing to do with it, and we must be vigilant at all times!'

Most of the older birds got very worked up at the words of the cara cara. They stared hard at the new arrival, throwing him threatening looks. One of the other kestrels leapt at the young bird and tried to claw him. The young kestrel called in a sharp *kee-kee-kee-kee* of alarm. He shuddered in fear, never having experienced a threat before. He didn't know what the problem was, and none of the birds was prepared to explain.

Why were they so agitated by his presence? he wondered. Why were they so angry with him? The young bird sat nervously on his perch, wishing he could be back in his mews. He wondered would all creatures be as hostile as these birds.

*   *   *

Night spilled over the falconry. A fox barked from a nearby field. The stars stood silent and watchful over a young bird's first night out in the open air.

CHAPTER 5

During the Hours of Darkness

A small bald man with glasses stood washing his hands at the stainless steel sink. The rats watched his every move. He walked over and opened a push-out window. Another man and a woman entered the laboratory. These were his assistants. The woman had a round, pleasant face and shoulder-length hair. The man was tall and thin with wavy grey hair cut short, and a pale, lined face. The woman was carrying a mug of coffee for Dr Thorpe.

'Thank you, Linda. Well, I'm afraid you were right. All dead. Probably killed during the night.'

'My God!' exclaimed Linda, 'The entire lot?'

'Yes. Fifty, against five. A massacre.'

'But it was expected,' argued her colleague, John. 'There would be no way that five could handle themselves against fifty wild rats, no matter how aggressive they were ...'

'But you don't understand,' said Dr Thorpe. 'The *five* killed the fifty ...'

'The five killed the fifty!' John exclaimed in amazement. 'The five we bred?'

'Yes indeed. It's astonishing,' Dr Thorpe replied. 'Come over and see for yourselves. It's not a pretty sight. Some of them have been cannibalised ...'

They looked into the glass case, where Natas and the four other rats scurried nervously over the mutilated bodies of the wild brown rats. The five were easily identifiable, as they were larger than the wild ones, and Linda had shaved a small star shape on their backs for easy identification. Natas sat with his back arched; another was hunched, tearing at the belly of a dead rat. Linda and the two men stared in stony silence.

'You're a right bunch of mean rats, no doubt about it,' Linda remarked, looking around the large case at the torn bodies of the dead animals, blood splashed on the glass and bits of fur scattered about. Some even had their heads torn completely off and several were half eaten from the obviously concentrated attack.

'We know now that they could easily clear an area of wild rats, without much trouble,' said Dr Thorpe. 'They've proved that they can be just as nasty and powerful as the ones we produced over a year ago.'

'The ones that escaped?' asked Linda.

'Don't remind me,' sighed Dr Thorpe. 'After attacking that technician, who almost died.'

'Yes,' said John. 'I remember coming back from holidays only to discover the place ransacked, and that poor fellow lying bleeding on the floor. Fericul and Rattus were their names, if I recall ...'

'Do you think they are still alive?' Linda pondered.

'No chance,' John replied. 'They were probably run over by a car or eaten by a cat. I don't think they could possibly have adapted to the wild after living in a glass case all their lives.'

Dr Thorpe was planning ahead. 'The next thing we need to concern ourselves with is to find out if they'll breed with wild ones, and what traits the offspring will develop ... would they become a menace if they were let go, even under controlled conditions? Well, that's all for another day. We need to clean up the mess and burn those corpses.'

White rabbits, mice and rats watched terrified from their cages as the two assistants proceeded to lift out the five rats, using heavily padded gloves, and place them in separate cages. Natas flared his nostrils and bared his teeth.

'You're a little devil,' said Linda.

'We need only keep two,' Dr Thorpe suggested. 'Put the others down tomorrow.'

* * *

When things were quiet and, apart from the security guard, the Nusham had gone home, Natas squealed to the other rats.

'Listen. We're getting out of here tonight. We're not going to end up dead meat, incinerated like the others!'

The other star rats agreed, but wondered how. One white rat asked if he could go with them. He had been used for different experiments to test his skill and knowledge.

'No,' said one of the star rats. 'We don't want some milky rat tagging along with us. He'd only draw attention to us.'

However, Natas thought about it and realised that this rat was very clever indeed and could be of some use to them. He decided to let him come along. If he proved to be a nuisance they could always kill him. The other white rats and mice kept quiet and just stared. They would be very happy to see the back of the star rats.

'Okay. Here's the plan. Are you listening?' snarled Natas. The star rats squealed and shivered with excitement and anticipation.

'We rock our cages until they fall to the floor. One of them at least should break open as a result. The first to escape releases the rest. Simple!'

The rats looked down to the floor of the laboratory. It seemed a long way to fall. They were petrified.

Fangs bared and feet clawing, Natas leaped and

heaved at the cage. It moved slightly. With more leaping and springing bounds he moved it yet again. The other rats were squirming now, writhing and hissing, urging him on. Natas fixed them with a stare, then lunged again at the thin bars. Still the cage moved only slightly. A shadow passed along the laboratory.

'It's the damn Nusham. Nobody move!' Natas whispered loudly.

The man looked in and shone his torch around the room. A monkey screamed from another room and a dog barked. The man turned and left. The rats could hear the rattle of keys as doors were being unlocked and re-locked.

'We'll have to wait until he goes for supper. It shouldn't be too long.'

They all sat hunched, listening to the footfall of the Nusham as he moved away from the laboratory towards his cabin. Everything was quiet again. Natas sat licking one of his paws, then paced up and down in the cage making a gritty sound. He twisted his body, eyes wild.

'No more living in a cage!' he cried. Narrowing his eyes he pressed his body against one side of the cage and with a charge of rage he flung his full weight at it. It shook, then, slowly tipping over, plunged and crashed to the floor.

The loud noise of the metal hitting the tiled floor startled all the animals. They screamed, stirred and shifted in their cages, absolutely petrified. There followed a deadly silence. The rats could see that the cage had landed upside down, but there was no sign of Natas.

The white rat pressed his wet muzzle through the thin bars and asked nervously: 'N–Natas, are you all right?'

There was no reply. The rats looked apprehensively at one another.

'Do you think he's ...?'

Then the snarling grunts of Natas could be heard. 'This damn cage is still closed. The rest of you get rocking now, do you hear me, or I'll tear the hearts out of every one of you!' he hissed.

There was an eruption of screeches and five cages began to move and rock. Then they too tumbled over and went crashing to the floor.

What the hell was that noise? the security guard wondered as he put down his mug of tea. Pushing back his chair he grabbed his torch and keys, and headed once more towards the laboratory.

'Are any of the cages open?' Natas asked anxiously.

'No,' said the star rats weakly.

'Mine is ...' said the white rat that had asked to escape with them.

'You *are* clever,' Natas grinned. 'Now, be a good rodent and release us before the Nusham gets back!'

The white rat quickly undid the latches and the doors sprang open.

'Well done, fellow rat. We appreciate what you have done and we won't forget it,' said Natas.

'Listen,' cried one of the star rats. 'The Nusham is

coming.' They could hear the hurried footfall on the path. The beam of the torch came through the window. 'Quickly, let's get out of here!'

The animals were all hissing or squealing, the monkey screaming loudly. Panicking, the rats scurried around the floor and hid behind boxes. They could hear an outside door opening and the keys being put in the laboratory door.

'What the blazes is happening here?' Examining the empty cages the security guard began to check under the table for the rats. Natas sprang at him. The others did likewise. The man got such a shock that he fell back and hit his head off a metal radiator, then lay silently on the floor. The torch rolled along the tiles.

Natas sniffed at the Nusham, then drew back and with the other rats scurried along the floor, looking for a way out. The white rat squealed and pointed to a small window that was open. Without hesitation they all scurried up along the desk, then straight up the wall, out through the small open window and down the outside wall to freedom! The other animals looked on, quivering and cowering in their dark cages.

CHAPTER 6

Trouble in Store

L ife was difficult for the young kestrel. He couldn't make friends with the other birds. They treated him with suspicion. He had no idea what he had done to warrant this treatment. When the Nusham flew the red-tailed hawk or the peregrine there was no comment. But when the falconer picked up the young kestrel there were whispers all around the falconry.

'See,' they would say. 'Look how he collaborates with the Nusham.'

Even in the evening the owls would be talking among themselves about him. Still, there was a lot to see from his perch – the visiting woodpigeon which would sit in the sprawling branches of the oak and preen or coo, and then clap his wings when he was flying away in a hurry; the swifts with their scythe-like wings wheeling and swooping in the sky, or the bees buzzing about the tall foxgloves near the ditch.

He became very nervous when the black cat patrolled the outskirts of the falconry, pacing across the wall, or sitting on its haunches, staring. Sometimes it would try and sneak over, but the sparrowhawk or the other kestrels would scream out in annoyance. This would set the guard dogs barking loudly. Then the Nusham would come out and yell at the cat or throw something at it. This was enough to drive it away, but it would never stray too far and many a time the kestrel watched the cat lie in ambush for some young chaffinch, robin or blackbird.

So many small birds met their end because of this black cat! The young kestrel knew he would not stand a chance if it came too near him.

He also had to contend with the kestrels that sat too close to him and were always trying to start a fight. One morning the racket became really bad, with the two of them screaming at him; the falconer came out and moved the young kestrel further up the falconry to where the griffon vulture used to be. The perch had been vacant for a long time.

'Now, I hope you won't get into trouble here.' The Nusham spoke testily. He then replaced the big perch with the one that the kestrel had been using on the lawn. 'No more trouble from you,' the Nusham said, wagging his finger, as he turned to walk towards the house.

The young kestrel settled nervously beside the golden eagle, who seemed so big and powerful, yet sat silently, paying scant attention to this new bird alongside him. The kestrel roused himself, preened a little, checked his tail feathers, then sat very still, feeling grateful to be away from the other kestrels and the cara cara. He looked around, regarding everything with curiosity, and a little fear, until he familiarised himself with it and assured himself of its safety.

The day wore on. There were no visiting Nusham so the birds felt relaxed. Remarks were passed about the fact that this young kestrel was now in the very place where Griff the vulture had perched.

'How dare he!' snapped the red-tailed hawk. 'Griff was so brave and proud.'

'And he used to tell such wonderful stories,' said the black kite, remembering the vulture with fondness. 'Now we have this creature trying to pass himself off as a bird.'

They began to flare up again.

'Settle down!' insisted the black vulture. 'We'll get to the bottom of it soon ...'

The cara cara waved down a magpie and they sat whispering.

*   *   *

The sun bathed the falconry in warm light. The golden eagle sat, shaded by the beech tree, nodding his head, half-dozing. Each day the eagle seemed to go deeper into his own thoughts. The young kestrel watched him. The eagle's eyes seemed lost among the brown feathers, but when a cranefly climbed the stem of some tall grass he opened them and they peered out, bright and glowing with life. There was a fire in his eyes, eyes that had searched the heather so long ago

for grouse or mountain hare – a young hunter on the wing. Then the eyes closed to slits, for that had been long long ago, in the green days of freedom.

The bateleur eagle stretched his wings. They glinted in the sunshine. When the young kestrel looked at him, this bird raised his crown feathers and adopted a threatening pose, then turned his back on him.

The birds started calling and flapping, some leaping from their perches: they knew food was on the way.

The falconer threw the food from a bucket. The tawny eagle mantled the dead day-old chicks and began to gulp them down quickly. Most of the owls were awake, though they wouldn't eat until darkness came. The golden eagle looked with indifference at his food, as it lay strewn about. Most of the food which had been left for him the day before was still there as well. Bluebottles and house flies wandered over the tiny yellow bodies ...

The exploding song from a wren on the boundary wall startled the young kestrel, then the golden eagle's eyes locked on his. They fixed on each other, the aged eagle and the nervous young bird. The eagle looked as if he was about to say something, but seemed to change his mind and turned away, leaving the thought unsaid. The young kestrel began to eat.

Suddenly from the sky came the magpies, crashing down upon him. The kestrel screeched in panic. The magpies leaped and pecked and hammered with their strong black bills on his back. The young kestrel flipped himself over on to his back and kicked out his feet, flailing with his talons. But the magpies were too clever and they stabbed and stabbed at him.

All eyes watched. The cara cara gloated as the magpies worked him over.

'Kill him!' he yelled loudly.

The young kestrel whimpered. The other birds concentrated on the fight, knowing full well that the young bird wouldn't stand a chance against the four attackers.

There was a sudden rush of large brown wings. They flapped furiously as the golden eagle roared: 'Let him be!'

The startled magpies stopped their vicious attack, realising that they were too close to the eagle for comfort. They stood, absolutely petrified. The falconry was tense with excitement, the young kestrel panting with fear. Raising his body higher, the eagle demanded to know who had put them up to it. The magpies stiffened with terror.

The eagle glared hard at them, then snapped again: 'Who put you up to this?'

'The cara cara,' they blurted out in chorus. 'He promised us his food rations for three days if we got him,' said the ringleader.

The eagle's eyes flashed menacingly. Flexing his talons and spreading his enormous wings, he lunged at the magpies, yelling at them to clear off and never to return. The magpies scarpered in fearful flight. The eagle stared long and hard in the direction of the cara cara who was cowering behind his perch; then turning, looked at the kestrel.

'Are you all right?' he enquired tenderly.

The young kestrel shook himself and nodded. The golden eagle bellowed out a warning: anyone who tried to harm this young bird again would have to answer to him. There was a deep silence.

'I have lived on this earth over thirty summers,' the eagle declared, 'and I can tell you here and now that, no matter how clever and cunning the Nusham are, they cannot create a bird's egg without a bird! This young bird here came from an egg like the rest of us. A wild egg. His wings are wild, like yours and mine, and some day he too will experience the freedom of flight! This much I promise, if it's the last thing I do.' He turned to the young kestrel. 'You were born for the sky,' he said quietly, 'and you'll go there soon.'

*   *   *

The other birds felt a lot calmer after the eagle's words. They settled down, watching dusk settle in.

'You must forgive them,' the golden eagle turned

again to the young kestrel. 'It's because of the tedium of being cooped up here like prisoners. They create their own fears and excitement to dull the pain of boredom. What's your name?'

The kestrel looked blank.

'You don't even have a name!' The golden eagle looked skyward. Stars winked in the celestial canopy. 'I am called "Capella". My clan comes from the high mountains across the seas. Mount Eagle is where our eyrie was.'

Scanning the wild sky he spoke softly into the night. 'Once we were all free in the sky together. We knew the mountains, trees and rivers. We soared, sailed and hunted. The land gave us food and shelter. Now we are old and tired. But our minds are not tired. We can remember the old days. We can say to each other: "Those days were good".' He gazed at the stars for a moment. 'Capella is descending in the north-west,' he said.

Looking at the kestrel in the faint light the golden eagle smiled. 'Of course, you don't know about those times. You don't understand my song. You were born within these walls. But I want to see you soar beyond this place. I want your wings to feel the wind beneath them. They are to become Wild Wings.'

The young kestrel looked pleased.

'You remind me of a young barn owl that escaped from here,' continued the golden eagle. 'He was called Kos. His brother Driad was here too. Yes! The night they escaped from here was a great night for all of us.'

'I'd like to leave here,' said the young kestrel forcefully.

'I'm glad to hear you say so,' said the golden eagle. 'Now, I'll give you a name and be proud of it. Vega is your name from now on. Capella is descending, Vega is rising.' These last words were whispered quietly.

The golden eagle turned again to the kestrel. 'Can you see Capella and Vega twinkling in the great silence?' the eagle asked.

An owl's hoot floated on the still air ...

CHAPTER 7

A Friend in Need

The birds in the falconry noticed how well the young kestrel was getting on with Capella, the golden eagle. They were glad about this because they could see that the eagle was back to his old self again, telling stories, eating and preening regularly. Every evening after the visiting Nusham had left, Vega and Capella would perch as close to each other as their cords would allow. Vega would hang on to every word spoken by the old eagle.

'I have so many memories and images,' Capella began one evening. 'They grow more precious each time I recall them and they comfort me when I'm feeling a sense of tedium. Hope rises again through these memories and I sit and reflect on those long-gone seasons. Vega, you must live your life so that you can collect these jewels for the mind. If you stay here in the falconry you'll have only a meagre exist-ence. There's no purpose, no meaning here, only emptiness. You must escape while you're still young.

I want to tell you all I know, then we'll plan your escape.'

Vega nodded. The eagle looked skyward.

'I soon will fly through the barriers of space and time,' he whispered, 'to where everything comes together in unity.'

The kestrel watched the golden tinge of sunlight on the eagle's head.

'Fling open your wings!' commanded Capella.

The kestrel obeyed.

'Let the warm breeze gather under them. It feels so good.' The eagle closed his eyes. 'I cast my mind back to when I was a young eagle, remembering my first flight, the endless vista of glens and rocky hills, winding rivers and dark lochs. I could hear the whoosh of my own wings as I lifted off – the panic I felt, then the relief knowing that my wings would support me. High I soared in wide effortless circles, using the warm air currents. I drifted without a wingbeat. Such freedom is impossible to describe!

'Then I was joined by my proud parents. We played, soared and spilled down the mountains, over the moors, then, flapping furiously to gain height again, we flew up into the wide skies through swirling clouds. Our eyrie was on a high plateau, known to our ancestors as Mount Eagle. I can still recall the tension I felt each time I lifted off from the cliffs to soar over the snow-clad mountain peaks.

'You too will know that tension and that delight, Vega. You must seek out the challenges of life and learn to face them; in that way you'll discover wisdom and understanding.' The old eagle lifted his foot in a stretch of talons, eyes glinting as he watched the sunlight streaming its shafts of golden yellow between the columns of trees.

Suddenly there was a movement through a tangled wall of nettles and a distinctive-looking creature broke cover, sniffed the air and scuttled across the rough grass. With his spiky back the hedgehog was recognisable to all except the kestrel, who had never laid eyes on such a creature before. It shuffled along the pebbled path, sniffing and searching incessantly for insects, worms and slugs. It stopped near the young kestrel and sniffed at him, then proceeded with a certain amount of confidence under the golden eagle's perch.

The eagle followed its every step. What a foolish creature, the kestrel thought. He sensed this spiky animal meant no harm to any of the birds in the falconry but he knew that the eagle's powerful feet could squeeze the very life out it. The golden eagle leapt from its perch and instantly the hedgehog curled itself into a ball. The eagle flipped it a little with its powerful bill and the ball of hedgehog rolled into a corner of a nearby hut.

How curious! Vega wondered how this creature could turn itself into a spiky ball. The eagle pressed his face close to the curled form and nudged it.

'Is that my old friend Hotchiwichi hiding in there?' he enquired.

The hedgehog slowly unravelled himself, then sniffed the face of the eagle.

'Hello, Capella. How've you been keeping?' the hedgehog enquired.

'Not too badly really,' replied the eagle, 'although I've been seeing visions of the Sky Place in my dreams and the Grey Owl beckons me to follow him.'

'You look well enough to me,' commented the hedgehog. 'Even though my eyes aren't as sharp as they used to be!'

'Have things been good with you?' enquired the eagle, back again on his perch.

'Oh very good. I wasn't disturbed during hibernation this time, thank heavens. Remember last season? I was nearly set ablaze by some Nusham when I slept beneath those leaves at the end of the garden! Why Nusham do things like that I'll never know. Still, they normally don't bother us except when we use their runs. Then they really get mad and drive over us with their travel machines.'

Hotchiwichi then looked with interest at the young kestrel and the old eagle introduced them. 'This is my young friend, Vega.'

'How do you do,' said the hedgehog. 'Vega ... That's a splendid name. Suits you very well. May your light shine brightly!'

The young kestrel beamed back gratefully.

'Well, I must go, Capella. I've a litter to keep an eye on. See you soon again.' And the hedgehog scuttled away across the long shadows.

'Well, it's time to sleep,' yawned the old eagle. He shuffled on his perch and settled down to rest. Vega too settled down to his dreams.

* * *

A light breeze ran through the darkness of the falconry. The black kite sat quietly on his block, wide awake, ruffling his feathers. He too wanted freedom, and having discovered a thin tear in his leash, had spent the whole night picking and pulling at the leather. Tomorrow he would be free! The other birds would be proud of him. He would be a hero. They would tell tales of him on long winter nights, while he flew over the great valleys and mountains of Africa.

Two full circles of the moon and he would be there. He had waited so long for this. He was fit enough, he convinced himself. If a swallow could manage it, so could he.

With that the jesses came away from the leather leash. He was free! His whole body trembled in

anticipation. He would wait until first light, then they'd all see him soaring into the sky, to freedom.

As morning was opening and the falconry gradually emerged from darkness, the black kite nervously looked around him. He purposefully preened his flight and tail feathers, staring hard at the other birds who were beginning to rouse themselves. His senses were keen, feathers bristling with anticipation, but his anxiety was deepening, sending shivers of fear through his body. It was now or never!

Trembling all over, the black kite raised his wings and flapped several times, panting nervously. The common buzzard stared at him as if sensing something. Then the bird bolted off his block and flew away over the tree tops. Startled eyes stared, bills snapping and wings flapping in excitement, as the silhouette of the black kite glided into the morning sky. Heads tilted skywards as the birds looked on, getting the last fleeting glimpse of a friend who was risking all for the freedom of the sky!

*   *   *

It was several hours before the falconer discovered that his prize bird was missing.

'Blast!' He kicked at the pebbled path in anger.

The dogs barked loudly, sensing his mood. The falconry was closed that day while the Nusham searched the area for his missing bird.

*　　*　　*

'He sure was a quiet one,' scoffed the cara cara, 'telling no-one of his plans to escape.'

'We would all do the same, given half a chance!' the peregrine retorted.

'I think it's wonderful,' offered Vega. 'The black kite was so lucky to get away.'

The golden eagle looked solemn. 'I hope he makes it. He's been here a long time.'

There was pain in the old eyes that fixed on the kestrel. 'He has seen many days of despair.'

Later, when the fuss had died down a little, the golden eagle spoke again to the young kestrel. 'Vega, you must prepare yourself for your escape now,' he said firmly and briskly. 'At first you'll be a stranger to the sky, then you will see the splendour of life, sharing in its mystery. It will bring you extraordinary knowledge. You'll lose the sense of isolation that we all feel here, the feeling of being banished from the sky. You will fulfil your true destiny.

'But beware of Nusham. They play havoc with the planet. Learn to fear.

Make friends, but watch out for enemies. Know the way of the winds. Tackle nothing you can't handle. Stick to small rodents, but don't be too proud to eat insects. Develop a sense of place.

'Take special care of your feathers. Feathers, especially the tail feathers, must be kept clean, otherwise their efficiency for flight and insulation become impaired. Don't worry too much if they get damaged, or you lose one. They will always grow again.

'Avail of dust baths if possible. Always roost high up in a tree or building and learn the art of staying motionless.'

Vega listened intently. The eagle's look became very gentle.

'You probably don't understand half of what I say, but some day it'll make sense, my little friend. Now, I think I'll rest a while.'

The black vulture had overheard and added his words of advice.

'He's right, little falcon. Heed his words well, especially about the Nusham. They have the death gun and the metal traps. They can move with awesome force against anything that's not Nusham – trees, birds, animals, rivers, seas, even their own kind. They are cruel beyond imagining. They want to reap the red harvest over all creation.'

CHAPTER 8

Ancient Memories

Black-furred bodies scurried among the dark shadows while traffic roared above the bridge. Bright lights pierced the night as trucks and cars thundered along, rushing to their destinations. Natas stopped to sniff the air, then decided to rest. He and the others sat, humped on their hindquarters.

'I love the darkness.' Natas flashed his long yellow incisors. 'It shields us from the prying eyes of our enemies, the dreaded Nusham. By the way,' he asked the white rat, 'what are you called?'

'Albino 57,' replied the white rat.

'What kind of dumb name is that?' enquired one of the star rats.

'Well, that's what the Nusham call me,' the white rat replied awkwardly.

'We'll have to give you a new name,' Natas sniggered. 'You look like a ghost, so maybe you should be called "Spook". How do you fancy that?'

'Oh, that s–suits me fine,' replied the white rat nervously.

The other rats laughed.

'You see. It suits you. Even my comrades approve of it!' Natas hissed loudly. 'Now, let's find some food. I'm ravenously hungry. I'm tired of eating scraps. Let's head for the park. I rather fancy some duck myself.'

With snouts twitching and fur stiffening the rats raised themselves on their haunches and looked around. Then they moved off towards the park. Spook kept a look-out as Natas and the others slipped into the chilly water, and glided past the water lilies to make their surprise attack on the mallards. Natas leapt on to a terror-stricken duck, caught her by the neck and wrenched the life out of her. His fearsome attack aroused the other rats' killing lust and they savaged three young drakes. A moorhen ran for cover.

Natas proceeded to devour his catch, snapping and gouging with razor-sharp teeth. The others began to tear

into their victims, spitting out feathers in their frenzied excitement to reach the flesh. Spook swam over to join them. He could smell the sweet odour of warm blood.

'Nothing tastes better than warm, moving flesh in one's jaws ...' Natas's eyes gleamed as he raised his bloody face from the duck's carcass. 'Who can describe the excitement of the kill!'

Then, narrowing his eyes he warned the others not to leave any remains. 'We don't want to arouse unwelcome attention.'

After they had eaten their fill they squealed triumphantly and swam back to the trees. There they shook themselves dry.

'It's time to move!' Natas yelled.

Quickly the other rats flanked him and they scurried to a deserted part of the city, where crumbling shells of buildings stood empty among rubble. They climbed a red-brick wall and ran along the top, keeping a constant look-out for feral cats and dogs.

Natas suddenly became aware of a bristle-furred creature below some floor-boards that lay across a mound of clay. Eyes glinting, he remarked: 'It's one of our own.'

The creature sat hunched, its snout twitching, sniffing the air. Its night-seeing eyes searched about for danger, then it moved off.

'Quick! After it!' commanded Natas.

They filed quickly along the wall until they reached the end and leapt on to the rubble. They approached cautiously as a pink scaly tail slithered through a gap in the wall, then disappeared.

The city rat trembled; he sensed he was being followed. He knew how a band of hungry rats could cannibalise one of their own kind. He cowered in the inner blackness of the basement floor. Outside he could see moving shapes. Thick furry bodies. Wood rattled, then the rats entered.

'Welcome,' the city rat whispered nervously.

Natas looked around with sharp eyes. 'Why are you hiding from us?' he asked.

The rat sat, mute. The others could sense that he was timid and fearful.

'All alone here?' Natas enquired, sniggering.

The city rat nodded. 'The Nusham have laid poison for us. Most of the clan in the area were killed off.'

'Well, it won't be long before the place will be re-colonised by rats from the surrounding areas,' offered Spook.

Natas glanced quickly at the albino rat, then said, almost cheerfully, 'Old Spook is the brains around here.'

The city rat offered them some food.

'Not tainted with poison I hope,' said Natas menacingly.

'No, of course not,' said the city rat.

They sat and ate sliced bread and lapped up fresh milk.

'I manage quite well on my own,' said the city rat, who by now was more relaxed.

The other rats quickly and greedily consumed the sliced pan.

'Where are you from?' enquired the city rat.

'We escaped from a laboratory. They were using us as "guinea pigs",' said Spook.

'That's good all right!' squealed the city rat. 'Using rats as guinea pigs! Some time ago another band of rats came by here. They escaped from one of those Nusham laboratories. Rattus came first. He was very interesting indeed. Stayed for several weeks. The elders of the clan liked him because he would bring the finest of foods for us each evening. Where he got it from is anyone's guess. The elders told him many of the clan secrets, all about the ancient land where Ratland existed. The Nusham built burial mounds above it.

'After a time a rat called Fericul came along. He was powerfully built. He spent several nights in the secret chambers with the elders. Then, on the night of the spring full moon, he declared himself Emperor. Some of the elders began to fear him. There was a lot of debating and quarrelling. The elders who were opposed to the Emperor disappeared mysteriously. Rumours spread that Fericul had actually killed them, but no-one dared to question the Emperor about it. By this time Rattus had been sent to find out about Ratland. He travelled by ship, then Fericul followed at the waning of the moon.

'Since that time, no news was ever heard of Fericul or Rattus. There were stories, of course, from travelling

rats, who said the Emperor had discovered Ratland.
Others said that he had killed Rattus and was living
in a city dump.

'I can tell you, we were all relieved to see the back
of the Emperor. I hope he was no relation of yours?'
the city rat added, suddenly sensing that Natas might
be a cousin.

'Are not all we rodents related?' remarked Spook.

No more was said. The rats moved out from the
dark cellar and stole among the ruins, seeking a
comfortable warm spot to rest. They chose a rambling,
derelict red-brick building, once inhabited by the
elders.

CHAPTER 9

Parting Friends

Take away this clouded veil
That lies between myself and the sky
Take away the fences strong
That wall my every way.
Take away these leather straps
That bind my very feet
Take away this heavy despair
That afflicts my weary heart.

Vega listened to the poetic words of the golden eagle.

'You must think me crazy,' Capella remarked, 'but I talk to my ancestors whose home is in the sky. I thank the One beyond the Sun for life.

'Remember, Vega, freedom must roar within you,' the old eagle, whose eyes seemed on fire, continued. 'Once we were wild. Now we are slaves. But we retain the wild spirit inside. Be proud. Remember we're

nothing when the spirit is gone. Let your spirit grow until it reaches the sky.'

Vega was deeply touched by the words of the golden eagle. Now, more than ever, the young kestrel sought to break from the clinging leather leash.

'Still no news about the black kite?' enquired the common buzzard.

'Sheila the heron would get word to us if anything went wrong. She's good like that,' remarked the tawny eagle.

'Look,' said the peregrine, 'the gates are opening. Here come more Nusham to gawk and stare.'

The birds sat still, talons gripping perches, scanning the onlookers with piercing eyes. The imperial eagle shivered, ruffled his feathers and called noisily at a young Nusham who poked him with a stick. The red-backed hawk amused himself by leaping furiously off his perch in the direction of the visitors. This startled the Nusham who moved quickly on. The snowy owls hissed menacingly when the Nusham peered through the laths at them, and the barred owls puffed themselves up and put on a threat display. The eagle owls usually did something similar and would throw in some bill-snapping for extra effect. But most times they just sat, indifferent to the spectators.

The falconer came out and flew the peregrine; this pleased the visitors. Watching her clearing the air, practising twirls, spiralling up into the sky, they could see the dark shadow chasing out from the sun, faster and faster, rending the air in mock attack, then coming down over the trees, skimming the heads of the other hawks, to land once more on the falconer's outstretched arm.

Afterwards the falconer let people stroke her slate-grey back as she sat on his gloved hand. The peregrine sat, tranquil and composed, while the visitors gazed into her deep brown eyes. The other birds couldn't figure out why the peregrine didn't fly away and escape. She always returned to the Nusham's fist, on command. The peregrine couldn't explain it either, but she said it was like an invisible cord pulling her back each time.

*   *   *

As the light faded and evening crept in, Vega noticed a strange white owl weaving silently over the trees. The ghostly white form could be seen clearly as it floated through the brooding shadows, then in and out through the deeper darkness of the trees until it alighted near to where Capella snoozed. There were many owls in the falconry, but none like this one.

The owl looked nervous. His feathers blew gently in

the breeze. He gave a whispered hiss, several times. Capella opened an eye, then both eyes widened as he saw his young friend Kos before him.

'Is this a dream?' he murmured, doubting what he saw.

'How are you, my good friend?' enquired the barn owl. 'It's been a long time!'

'Too long,' said Capella. 'Well, you look strong, Kos. All grown-up and thriving, I see.' The old eagle seemed overwhelmed with emotion, and tears welled up in his eyes.

There were many questions asked. Kos explained that he had lacked the courage to come back to the falconry until now.

'Nothing changes much around here,' said Capella, 'except that we get older. The occasional injured bird is brought in, damaged by overhead wires, or shot. You've seen it all, I'm sure. The black kite escaped recently. Do you remember him?'

'Indeed I do,' said Kos. 'I hope he's managing okay out there.'

The other birds became quite excited when they realised Kos had returned. They were all wide awake, straining to hear the conversation. Kos told them the saga of the rats, how he had been trapped in Ratland, and all about his visit to the Sacred Cliffs. The birds had heard of the recent increase in rat activity. Some rats actually pinched food from the falconry, according to the eagle owl, who saw everything.

When Kos spoke about the Sacred Feather, now in safe keeping and guarded by the Council of Ravens, they sat in awe. They were elated and overwhelmed by what had happened to him. All through the night he regaled them with his treasury of stories.

'We'll live on these stories for a long time,' the black vulture finally declared. 'They'll be recalled and recounted over and over again. You've done us proud, Kos! We all feel so alive because you've come back to share these experiences with us.'

Kos felt a little embarrassed, but he was glad he had made the effort to visit the falconry. He was glad too that all the things which had happened, however bad, could be used to cheer up old friends. He told them about Driad and Snowdrop and their successful brood, and of his own partner, Crannóg.

'It's good to have a partner,' commented the eagle owl. 'It'll shelter you from loneliness.'

* * *

With the faintest glimmer of first light a blackbird sounded his piping song, heralding the morning. Kos was urged by his friends to leave quickly; they didn't want the Nusham to catch him again!

There was an air of contentment in the falconry after he was gone. Vega hadn't managed to get an introduction, but he liked the owl and his amazing stories. He now sat watching starlings pour across the sky and settle on a nearby pylon.

Capella was basking in the warm sun. He seemed absorbed in his own thoughts. Then he threw a glance at Vega.

'Forgive me for not introducing you to young Kos,' he said. 'Time didn't allow it. It did my heart good to see him again, though. You and he are the best thing to happen to me for a long time.' His voice became feeble as he continued.

'Soon I'll make my escape from the confines of this falconry. All any wildfolk can hope for is a clean death. I can hear the wind singing in my wings. I'll go to a land of undisturbed harmony ...'

Vega became anxious. He could see the strange jerking of the old eagle's body.

'I feel a deep burning in my throat. Things are becoming dizzy,' murmured Capella. He stiffened. 'It's all right, my little friend. I'm not afraid. I return to the infinite reservoir from which all life springs. While some flow out others flow back in. The tedium of waiting is nearly over, Vega. Here's my last wish for you –

'May the seasons treat you well
May you soar joyfully on warm winds
May you be gifted with good friends
May you live life well
And may the earth mother
Be proud of your life ...'

After chanting these soothing words, Capella assumed the stillness of stone. 'I am close to death,' he murmured. 'The Grey Owl calls ...'

Vega felt helpless. He saw a glazed look come over the ancient eyes. The other birds shuddered as they watched their old friend slipping away.

At last, calling up his last reserve of strength, Capella whispered to his young friend: 'You must escape from here soon ... before it's too late. You're now strong and ready.'

Then he slumped back and was gone. His dark brown body stiffened as he lay on the ground below the perch.

* * *

Death stalked the falconry twice that day. In the evening a Nusham brought back the corpse of another bird. It was that of the brave black kite. He had flown into some overhead wires and been electrocuted.

'Life crumbles like dust beneath our feet,' sighed the black vulture, while the barred owls chanted in unison:

> 'Fly now, radiant birds
> Back to the bright sky of forever ...'

That evening a heavy rain fell.

CHAPTER 10

Dangerous Visitors

A clap of distant thunder startled Hack, the one-eyed rat, as he moved out from his dark shelter. He sniffed the air nervously, sensing something was about to happen. The other rats were below ground, hidden in the tunnels of the city.

A flash of lightning briefly illuminated the city dump. This was followed by an explosive roar of thunder that made Hack tremble. He crept on stealthily, sniffing the air, his one eye ever-watchful, feeling even more apprehensive as he moved through the grey light.

There was a small movement. He thought he saw a white rat. Was it a ghost? Was it the storm that was making him so nervous? he wondered.

Sheet lightning lit up the sky, framing an old fridge. Four large dark rats and a white rat were clearly visible. Hack backed away nervously, then he turned sharply, ready to make a run for it. Behind him stood another dark rat, glaring.

'Fericul!' Hack screamed in terror. 'But you're dead!'

Hack tried to make a run for it, but Natas caught hold of his scaly tail.

'That's no way to treat visitors,' he sniggered. 'Especially when one of them is the Emperor's true heir.' He stared into Hack's good eye. 'Do you know the smell of death?' he asked.

'No–I mean, yes,' blurted Hack.

Natas grabbed Hack by the throat. 'You have a choice,' he hissed. 'You can help us or I'll wrench the life out of you. Do I make myself clear?'

'Very clear,' said Hack. 'I'd be delighted to help such a prince among rats.'

'A prince,' said Natas, 'I like that. You learn fast. I think we will get on fine.'

The storm was now raging all around and heavy rain lashed them.

'Care for some shelter?' Hack nervously asked.

Natas nodded, the other rats leaped from the fridge, and they followed Hack underground.

*   *   *

Hack shifted uncomfortably on his haunches as he introduced His Royal Highness Prince Natas, the Prince's albino adviser Spook, and the star rats. The hoard of black and brown rats sat about, squealing and whirling in frenzied excitement. Some of them, remembering the Emperor Fericul, were very apprehensive. The younger ones were impressed by these large creatures with the star symbol on their backs.

'Perhaps the Prince would care to say a few words,' suggested Hack, feeling a little more relaxed at this point.

Natas immediately took centre stage. 'My comrades,' he began, 'thank you for your hospitality at such short notice. I can tell you, my subjects and I are glad to be in from that storm. Most of you remember the Emperor Fericul, a noble rat, with vast plans for the rodents of the world! His vision, unfortunately, was not realised. Well, I have a vision too, my comrades, a world free of our enemies.'

There was great cheering from the other rats. Natas continued: 'The world, my comrades, has fallen on evil times. The Nusham has incessantly plagued the earth with dangerous ideas and the spectre of pollution. All creatures know this. He has started the march of death for all creatures. Can we allow this?'

Angry screams of 'No!' echoed through the tunnels.

'I've come not only as a leader, but also as a friend,' declared Natas. 'I know you don't ask for much out of life – a warm dry place to lay your head and a full belly. But our enemies want to take even those small pleasures away from us. We simply cannot allow this! I know the ancient site of Ratland was discovered and defiled by our enemies ... Well, I want to restore it to its proper glory!'

There were loud cheers of approval from the attentive listeners.

Spike, a close friend of Hack's, whispered in his ear: 'Echoes of the old Emperor, don't you think?'

'Shush,' said Hack, for he could see that Spook was watching them.

'Well, my comrades, I don't want to detain you much longer,' Natas concluded. 'We're exhausted from our long voyage, but it was worth it. We met many a fellow rodent who filled in all the blanks about the great Emperor Fericul's mission. I promise you, my comrades, with your help we'll succeed. Now, we'll rest.'

There was more great cheering. Hack ordered food to be brought for the distinguished guests – ham slices, bread, cheese and sweet biscuits, all served with plenty of cool milk. Natas was pleased indeed.

'I'd like you to have a banquet in my honour,' he said, 'and invite all the rodents in the area and surrounding countryside.'

Hack agreed, he knew it would be crazy to refuse.

'The Emperor Fericul had a banquet too,' remarked Spike. Natas gave him a cold-blooded stare and Spike quickly added: 'Great minds think along the same lines.'

*   *   *

The eerie light of a waning moon appears as night shrouds the land. Huddled in large packs, sleek black rats emerge from dark dwellings and scurry purposefully towards the city dump. House mice tentatively follow. High-pitched squeals of pigmy shrews can be heard as they leave the security of the fields. Excitement mounts as a river of night creatures moves over the debris, sniffing in frenzied anticipation – black, brown and grey furred bodies flooding into the city dump from every direction, squirming, wriggling, scuttling, scrambling. The ground shivers with movement. The rodents have arrived.

Hack tenses himself as he welcomes them all. There's a sweet smell in the air of bacon, cheese, bread, fruits and rodents. Faint is the tainted smell of Nusham. The city dump belongs to the rats. Squatting on their haunches in the rubble, claws splayed and tails wriggling, they watch and wait, senses keen, bristling with expectation, to set eyes upon the Prince of Darkness – Natas – and his star pack.

*   *   *

Spike and Hack were very pleased with the enormous turn-out. The banquet was prepared. The guests had arrived. However, as yet there was no sign of Natas, Spook or the star rats. In fact they had not been seen for several days.

After waiting for a number of hours the rodents began to grumble and demanded to see Prince Natas. Hack suggested they all feast. Prince Natas was a very important rodent, he said, and had business to attend to, but he would be along shortly. They relaxed and tucked into the fine banquet prepared by the city-dump rats committee.

Suddenly, monstrous shadows were cast across the clearing. Hack sniffed, wrinkled his nose and drew back in horror. He could see large bulging shapes and yellow eyes that smouldered in the darkness.

'Cats!' he screamed at the top of his voice.

Squeals of panic rang out from terrified rodents.

'We're all done for!' some yelled.

'It's a trap!' others shouted, as they dived for cover.

'Run for your lives!' screamed the mice.

On the bonnet of an abandoned car stood Natas, Spook and the star rats.

'Have no fear, comrades!' shouted Natas.

The rodents shook with terror as they saw more than twenty marauding cats with arched backs seated on the ground beside the car. Tensely concentrated, and with fixed gazes, the rodents tried to comprehend the situation. The cats just stared back. Twisted forms straightened as Natas spoke.

'I hope you're enjoying yourselves, and that there's full and plenty for everyone. First, allow me to introduce myself. I'm Prince Natas. These are my loyal star rats and Spook here is my spokesrodent and adviser. I have come to liberate you from your enemies and yourselves ...'

The rodents sat listening quietly, but kept a watchful eye on the cats.

'... I've come from the same royal line as the Emperor Fericul, indeed from the very same place. I come to continue his great mission, to restore Ratland to its former glory! We are a glorious race of creatures.

We should be living like the noble race we are, but instead we live in sewers, dumps, city ports, neglected fields, crumbling buildings and river banks, existing from one meal to the next, forever watching over our shoulders for an attack by our enemies – owls, hawks, dogs, stoats, foxes, badgers, minks, others ... the list is endless! And, of course, the Nusham with his poisons and traps–'

'Not forgetting cats,' squealed a pigmy shrew.

There was a deadly silence. The rodents shifted, squirmed and wriggled nervously. All eyes turned towards the shrew.

'Well, it's true,' said the pigmy shrew, trembling all over. Natas's eyes glinted with malice, teeth bared. Then he broke into a malevolent grin.

'Cats,' he hissed. 'Of course, you're right. Cats have been our enemies, some of them, that is.'

Natas slid down from the bonnet of the car and roamed among his listeners. The rodents shifted cautiously on their haunches, watching his unfriendly and accusing eyes. He came close to the pigmy shrew and glowered fiercely. The shrew retreated, terrified.

Settling on a car tyre, Natas continued.

'I'd like to introduce some friends – the city cats. We met recently, quite by chance, and discovered we could be of mutual benefit to each other. Their proud leader is Moloch.'

A large black cat with a long scar across his face stood up. He smiled, drawing his lips back to expose his teeth in a chilling grin, then slunk back to his sitting position. The rodents, ears pricked, stayed desperately alert.

Hack watched the line of cats. He could feel their quiet aggression, though their eyes were expressionless slits. He knew they were professional killers, sizing up the situation. Yet, if they did attack they wouldn't stand a chance against so many rodents. He also knew that Natas was no fool and had plans for them.

'These cats are not the pets of Nusham, sources of pleasure, killing a few birds,' continued Natas. 'No, these are the ones that have abandoned their cosy Nusham homes. They live like us in the city dump, in alleys, yards and vacant Nusham houses. They are seldom seen and Nusham do not know their numbers.

'These cats can take down rabbits, pheasants and ground-nesting birds. They're the greatest destroyers of wild birds after the Nusham. And they excel themselves in springtime, when the young birds are leaving their nests. Our feline neighbours have offered to help us destroy our enemies and share in the great victory.

'I don't worry too much about Nusham. They've lost their way in life. They spend all their time producing vast and complex machines to boost their own egos and to accumulate wealth. Their lives have been thrown into confusion and darkness. But they've no real knowledge of the darkness. However, I have, my comrades, and I'll teach you to descend to the riches of dark thought. We must put an end to tenderness and replace it with the brutalising powers of darkness! My comrades, we must allow all cruelty, all sadistic tendencies to rise up from within. Only then we can truly become the "Super Beast"!'

A squeal of terror came from a female rat, nursing her new-born litter.

'I can't believe what I'm hearing,' she sobbed, 'Surely cruelty and violence have tarnished all creatures. The only real hope for us is to leave these dreadful ideas behind so that all creatures may one day co-exist in harmony and true freedom.'

Spike slithered over to the female who had spoken so passionately.

'Quiet,' he whispered. 'I warn you for the sake of your family. You don't know what you're dealing with here. He wouldn't think twice of sinking his teeth into your pretty neck.'

Natas grimaced in sheer hatred. The younger rats booed and hissed at the young mother.

Natas spoke again, 'I understand your fears but you've nothing to be concerned about. We'll take care of everything. All we ask of you here is obedience and loyalty.'

'It's getting late!' Spook spoke to the assembled rats. 'The Prince must rest. He's delighted with such a vast turnout. Eat, drink and be merry, comrades, and may the darkness get you safely home!'

Natas looked at the star rats and grinned slyly.

'They're a pushover.'

CHAPTER 11

Freedom in the Air

The morning was fresh and cool. A mournful aura hung about the falconry like a clinging fog. The birds sat in silence. They hadn't eaten for three days as a mark of respect to the golden eagle.

Vega woke each morning expecting to see his old friend Capella sitting there. The perch stood so empty and silent. Bluebottles wandered over the white-splashed place where once the noble bird had sat. Below, at the base of the perch, a few brown feathers lay scattered around; these were the only remaining traces of the great Capella.

A thrush alighted on a rowan tree and obliged with a virtuosity of song that broke the haunting silence.

Fixing a curious eye on it the black vulture spoke softly: 'We must always hope anew each morning, whatever yesterday's despair. That's what Capella once said to us, after we lost the griffon vulture.'

Trundling through a gap at the base of the old stone wall came Hotchiwichi. His ground-hugging body moved with great speed along the path. 'Salutations, feathered friends!'

There was a stare of recognition from Vega.

'I can't stay long,' sighed the hedgehog. 'I hope the Nusham is not about.'

The black vulture shook his head.

'Good,' said Hotchiwichi. He sniffed at the old eagle's perch. 'Poor Capella will be sorely missed, and the black kite too. What a shame.'

'How did you find out?' asked the black vulture.

'Well, a robin informed us on the dawn chorus several days ago,' replied Hotchiwichi. 'We hear most things that way. I would have come sooner but I fell through a cattle grid, and couldn't get out again. Only for old Crag, the fox, I wouldn't have been able to carry out old Capella's last request. Crag pushed down a hazel branch so that I could climb out. Well, no time to lose. I'd better hurry ...' he muttered to himself.

Vega looked blankly at the black vulture, who seemed to know more than he was letting on. The hedgehog drove his muzzle behind Vega's perch, fastened his mouth over the thin leather leash, and began to chew and gnaw at it.

A door opened and the falconer stepped out. He stretched his arms over his head and gave a loud yawn.

'Hurry!' yelled the bateleur eagle in a rasping voice. 'The Nusham is awake.'

The cara cara called nervously in alarm.

'Quiet!' said the common buzzard. 'You'll only catch the Nusham's attention.'

Vega tried to control his trembling body as he watched the hedgehog chewing away at the leash.

'It's done!' cried the hedgehog, beaming with pride. Saliva ran from his mouth.

The falconer walked towards the kennels with food for the dogs, not noticing the spiky mammal scurrying away down the path and out through a gap in the wall. Gates creaked and clattered as the falconer left the kennels and strolled through the falconry. He stopped and checked each bird as he passed by. Vega swivelled his head, his eyes searching the sky.

'Make a bolt for it now!' ordered the black vulture.

The Nusham came closer, the birds looked on and the tension became unbearable. Surely the Nusham would notice the broken leash! Vega felt paralysed for a moment, then he suddenly flung open his wings, and arched them back. Capella's words rang in his head: 'Freedom must roar within you!' With a sudden rush of pointed wings he leapt from his perch and flew into the freedom of the air.

'Goodbye, old friends,' he called, as he soared higher, skimming and floating over the tree tops.

The startled Nusham watched in disbelief as the young kestrel planed overhead, then flew away beyond the line of trees that surrounded the falconry. The birds shrieked and called, beating their wings in support.

Vega alighted some distance away on a larch tree. His heart was pounding, his body trembling. He could hardly believe it. This was freedom, to fly anywhere he might choose, to perch anywhere he wished and rest in any tree he desired!

Wide-eyed he looked back. He could see the beech trees of the falconry in the distance. They looked so beautiful, yet who would know by looking at them that they masked a bird prison. He shuddered at the thought, having now tasted the first moments of freedom.

Scanning the area he could see the meadows stretching out before him – hedgerows of hawthorn, some rowan trees, holly and white alder bordered the fields. A hare moved through the hedge and across the open field. It stopped to nibble at sweet clover, sat upright on its hunkers to look around briefly and then bounded away.

Dogs barked and to his horror Vega could see the falconer and his dogs crossing the fields and heading in his direction.

The falconer didn't hold out too much hope of

catching the bird. He wasn't too concerned about losing a kestrel but he had a fondness for this one because of the circumstances surrounding its birth. He sorely missed the golden eagle and the black kite, both gone in the one week.

The dogs barked and rushed forward. But just then Vega lifted off on pointed wings and flew away. The falconer knew that he had lost his kestrel. He wondered would it survive in the wild. He regretted not training it and passing it on to some young enthusiastic would-be falconer. Over the years several teenagers had asked him for birds. He usually gave them an injured one to see how they managed the care of a bird; then when they were ready he'd give them a hawk or a kestrel. But now that this kestrel had tasted freedom he knew that he'd never see it again.

*   *   *

Vega flew onwards until he reached an old mill by the river. There he rested, preened a little and picked at the remaining leash until it pulled out through the brass eyes of the jesses. He also tried hard to peck off the jesses but they were too securely fastened to his legs. As he ruffled his feathers the young kestrel looked out on his new world. The movement of the water began to fascinate him, the oily glassiness which twisted and played around the stones, the swaying and swooning motions of the water weed. It became a living thing with a life of its own, on its own special journey. Suddenly a fish broke the surface, making great expanding circles.

Further down a heron flapped heavily towards the river. Vega decided to take to the air.

Lifting off from the lichen-covered wall, he cruised effortlessly upwards, soaring and circling higher and higher. Then, wheeling eastwards, he levelled out over the soft grasslands. Across the peaceful landscape he sailed, scanning the patchwork fields below, all neatly hemmed with hedgerows.

Autumn had touched the trees with its mysterious alchemy. Olive greens were tinted golden, copper beech leaves had changed to orange, oak leaves were dyed deep bronze and sycamore leaves had turned to scarlet. Berries dressed the hedgerows and glistened and sparkled like jewels from every bough and twig. Flowering heads of honeysuckle pushed through the matted tangle of brambles.

A handsome male blackbird perched on a bramble bush, attracted by its soft berries. Its glossy black plumage shone in the sunlight as it feasted contentedly, pecking the juicy berries and gulping them down.

Ox-eye daisies bathed in the light of an autumn sun and crab spiders climbed through their creamy-white petals to hide in ambush for their prey. Young rabbits emerged to feed on the lush supply of vegetation.

Vega, flying close to all this activity, suddenly caught sight of a black and white flash of wings. He turned and saw a large family of magpies cocking their tails as they dropped to the ground in search of food. The young kestrel decided to give them a wide berth and quickly flapped away, climbing higher into the sky. He felt as if he had dissolved into the air and become one with the sky and the wind.

Stopping to hover on a gentle breeze, with tail fanned, he hung in the sky and marvelled at his colourful world. He fixed his gaze as more rabbits hopped with delight around a meadow, while others cowered in a thistle patch. As the golden light from the fading sun streaked the sky Vega side-slipped and dived from the sky, skimming low over the fields. He headed back towards the old mill which he felt would be a safe roost for the night.

Alighting on an old exposed beam he settled himself close to the wall, his mind storing up all that had happened to him during his first great day of freedom. His thoughts slipped back to Capella, and to all his friends at the falconry; then forward, to life, to adventure. At last, happy and drowsy, he drifted into a deep, deep sleep.

CHAPTER 12

Ratland Revisited!

A silver moon hangs waning in the ebony night sky. On the fringes of the bog lifeless trees stand in grave-like stillness, their twisted forms caressing a dense fog that seeps over the land. Alert eyes dart fearfully about the stark and cheerless place. Natas moves menacingly through the undergrowth. The star rats seem as petrified with fear as Spook is.

'Is it much further?' enquires Spook.

'Nearly there,' replies Hack, remembering the terror of his first visit to this alien place.

Large moss-covered stones stand tall and mysterious beyond the gnarled trees on the hill.

'At last,' sighs Natas, prowling around the ancient tomb. Sniffing along the crumbling walls, he comes to a cobweb-enshrouded hole.

'Here's a way in,' he yells, sticking his snout through the cobweb. A strong musty smell comes from the deserted tomb. A spider hurries towards his web but Natas snaps at it, crunching up its soft brown body.

The other rats move reluctantly closer and follow the Prince into the abode of the dead. Their bodies merge with the shadows, scrambling down the large passageways into the chambers where the ancient Nusham are laid to rest. Scurrying along the stone passageway, Spook shrieks in terror as he stumbles upon the skull and bones of a Nusham. The others make a bolt for the exit.

'Come back,' yells Natas. 'Afraid of a heap of bones? If it were a live Nusham then you might have cause to worry but this ...' he sniggers slightly, climbs onto the skull and rests on his haunches.

'It seems we can't go any further,' he announces, staring coldly at the others. 'The tunnel below is completely blocked. The secret passage has to be excavated and cleared of stones and rubble.'

*　　*　　*

Hack had told Natas of the battle in Ratland – how their enemies had come to rescue one of their own. But he didn't mention that it was Spike and himself who had arranged this cave-in to trap their enemies! Although the cave-in had ended the battle, their enemies had escaped, taking Emperor Fericul with them.

'It'd be a very difficult task to clear the passage,' remarked Spook. 'Thousands of rodents would be needed and it'd take a long time. So many rodents working around the moon would very soon be noticed by our enemies, especially the Nusham!'

Natas paced up and down in the dreary darkness.

'Well, Spook, any bright ideas for solving this problem?'

The white rat scratched nervously and pulled at his whiskers. 'If we could get help from another source ...'

'Continue,' urged Natas excited.

'Rabbits!' said Spook. 'Rabbits. They could clear the dirt-filled tunnels in one evening.'

Natas narrowed his eyes. 'That's an *excellent* idea. Now, how do we convince them to help us?'

Spook looked at the star rats. They just stared back with blank expressions. Hack suggested that it might be possible to get the co-operation of the rabbits by instilling in them some kind of fear; maybe hinting that a deadly new disease would strike their warren and that the ancient tomb was a secure place where they would be safe.

'Oh, good, very good!' said Natas. 'What kind of disease had you in mind?'

'Maybe something like the dreaded myxomatosis, only worse. That'd be sure to do it!' replied Hack.

'Oh, I like it, I like it,' Natas grinned. 'Now, how do we spread this fear to the nearby warren?'

'Rabbits are very dumb creatures,' said Hack. 'It wouldn't take much to spook them into doing our will.'

Natas looked at Hack, 'A clever choice of words – spook them! Yes, a ghost from the past! That's the answer.' Then turning to Spook, the white rat, he said: 'Tomorrow, just after nightfall, you will present yourself as an ancestor from the past who has come to warn the rabbits of a terrible disaster which is about to befall them. Hack will arrange that all the rabbits of this area are here to listen to you–'

'That might prove somewhat difficult,' interrupted Hack.

Natas's eyes seemed charged with violence. 'It could prove *fatal* if it's not achieved.'

Hack backed away nervously from the Prince.

'I think we have a ghost of a chance!' murmured Spook in a nervous attempt to break the tension. This brought loud laughter from Natas and the star rats.

*　　*　　*

Hack sat in the dark seclusion of a hedge and watched the rabbits emerge from their burrows into the fading light. They appeared to be alert and wary as they began to feed on the moist grass.

Suddenly a loud squeal came from the hedge. The rabbits turned nervously, ears erect. Some made a bolt for the security of their warren. The others sat up on their haunches, staring and twitching.

Hack staggered out, jerking and swaying from side to side, until he collapsed in a heap near the rabbits. The rabbits twitched their whiskers and sniffed at him. He shuddered as if in dire agony, then became still and appeared lifeless.

The rabbits circled Hack. The leader, Cuniculus, came over. 'What's up?' he demanded.

Hack opened his one eye. 'I've just seen a ghost ...'

The rabbits recoiled in horror. Their leader looked on with suspicion; he didn't trust rats. 'Prove it!' he said.

Hack shot up. 'Back there, at the ancient burial mound ...' He pointed to the place.

The other rabbits gathered round the rat. Hack knew they were filled with a mixture of curiosity and fear.

'I'll go back if you all come with me.'

The rabbits consulted among themselves for some time, squatting close to the ground. At last, their leader agreed to follow the one-eyed rat.

* * *

Spook sat anxiously at the entrance to the tomb. He could see the fog creeping like a grey shroud across the landscape. Two star rats remained behind with him, but Natas had left. He was to return later that night. Spook circled around the tunnel. He didn't really like the star rats but he was glad of their company. He didn't fancy spending a night alone in the company of bones.

Peering into the gloom, Spook could see the rabbits coming up the hill. Hack stopped near the giant stones, squealing loudly. He pointed.

'That's the spot,' he yelled, hoping Spook could hear him.

The rabbits sat, ears erect, trembling with anticipation. They watched and waited, ears primed for sounds, but nothing stirred. The leader, Cuniculus, began to dismiss the whole notion as nonsense. 'Let's go,' he suggested.

'Look! There!' yelled a terrified rabbit, as he watched a white ghost-like form of a rat appear through the seeping fog.

'Do not be afraid ...' said Spook, with a quiver in his voice. 'I come to do you no harm ... but to warn you!' He sat on his haunches close to the entrance hole, while the two star rats stayed hidden behind in the shadows.

The rabbits stood around in silence, like frozen forms.

'I have come from the caverns of darkness ... to warn you ...' Spook heaved a deep sigh. 'You are all in danger ...'

The rabbits trembled, their anxiety deepening.

'A death-tightening grip is clutching at all species,' Spook continued. 'The Nusham want to turn the land into wastelands of desolation. They've launched a crusade of hate. Death will stalk the land, my comrades. The red plague will strike you all, far worse than the swollen eyes disease. The Nusham want to make ghosts of you all. I can see your warrens destroyed, the floors stained ... with blood!'

'What are we to do?' pleaded Cuniculus, sensing the mounting fear around him.

*   *   *

Shadowy forms moved through the bog, sinking down on all fours with bellies easing to the ground. Lurking and listening deep in the long grasses, Natas, the star rats and the feral cats had returned.

*   *   *

Spook convinced the rabbits that they must use the ancient burial mound as a shelter in times of danger. Only then would they be safe, he warned them. Then he retreated slowly, backing into the tunnel and hiding in one of the chambers alongside the two star rats.

'Did you see how he evaporated?' suggested Hack, 'Like the fog. We must heed his warning. We can't ignore a message from beyond the grave.'

'You're right,' said Cuniculus. 'We'll come here tomorrow and investigate the inside of this ancient place.'

'With the greatest of respect I think we should investigate it now,' said Hack. 'Tomorrow may be too late.'

'If you go in first,' suggested one of the rabbits.

Hack feigned fear, then with hind quarters trembling he agreed. He entered cautiously, followed by four buck rabbits.

Just then a trembling voice echoed through the tunnels. It was Spook, issuing instructions: 'You must clear the entrance to the lower chambers. Do it now, before it's ... too late. Farewell!'

The four buck rabbits squealed in terror at the sound of the voice. 'Let's get out of here,' shouted one. They made a bolt for the exit.

Outside they told Cuniculus what they had heard. Without further hesitation, Cuniculus ordered that they all enter the tomb and clear the passageways without delay.

*　　*　　*

Hack sat outside, below a large stone, watching the rabbits burrow their way into the lower chambers. Heaving and pushing they removed the clay and old roots. Rodent skulls and bones were carefully packed back into the walls. Tugging and pulling, the rabbits worked all through the night. Before first light they had cleared the tunnel.

When Cuniculus entered he saw the large stone with a rodent carved into it.

'This place is Ratland!' he exclaimed to Hack. 'Your ancient home. How come you never told us this before?'

'I didn't know,' said Hack. 'Honest. But it'll be a safe haven for your kind too. Trust me.'

The rabbits decided to leave and shake the dust of the burial tomb from their fur. But as they emerged into daylight Natas and the star rats were sitting there, ready for action.

'Salutations!' said Natas. 'I like to thank you and your dedicated workers for clearing the tunnels.'

'Who are you?' demanded Cuniculus.

'I'm Prince Natas. These rodents are my subjects. I will soon be enthroned in my kingdom, thanks to you and your long-eared friends. You'll be rewarded for this great deed!'

'What's going on?' demanded the rabbit leader. 'We came here because of a warning from a ghost rodent.'

'What's the matter?' sniggered Natas. 'Do you smell a rat?'

Cuniculus realised he'd been deceived. 'I've a good mind to set my bucks on you.'

Just then Spook emerged from the burial mound, followed by the two star rats.

'Let's get out of here!' shouted the leader. 'We've been made fools of by these slimy rodents.'

The rabbits grouped together and hopped away down the hill.

Natas's hackles rose, anger flashing in his eyes. Then his anger turned to admiration.

'Well done, Spook, you've served me well. I won't forget it.'

'Glad to be of service,' said Spook proudly. 'Only

for the rabbits we couldn't have done it.'

'They've served their purpose. Soon they'll be cat food,' Natas sniggered as he watched their retreating forms.

'Oh no,' said Spook, 'I don't think they should be killed. It doesn't seem right.'

Natas's eyes narrowed, then he thrust his face up close to Spook's. There was a deadly silence. Natas flashed his yellow incisors.

'You're a rat of principles, I see.'

The star rats circled him. Hack backed away.

'I have my principles,' blurted Spook. 'But if you don't like them I'll find some new ones!'

The star rats squealed with laughter. Natas sat back on his haunches. 'Your wits have saved you, dear Spook – but don't push your luck.'

Suddenly, squeals and screams of panic rent the air. The cries travelled up from the bottom of the hill. They were the cries of terrified rabbits. The wild cats were at work. Teeth slashed into skin, tearing away at furry coats. Claws raked and jaws clamped around necks. Razor teeth gouged out flesh. Soon the screams ebbed away and a terrible silence hung over the place.

'It seems the ambush has gone according to plan,' grinned Natas. 'We'll all dine on rabbit tonight!'

CHAPTER 13

Dangers in the Wild

In the purity of the morning light Vega soared high into the sky. Veering to the right he could see below him starlings feeding in stubble. He began to sweep down, graceful and nimble, towards the fields. Over blackberry briars he flew, scanning overgrown nettles for any movement. He was feeling ravenous. He hadn't managed to catch a worthwhile meal for days, feeding mainly on crane flies, some common grasshoppers, several cockchafers and a damselfly. He'd even tried a slug. The taste was hateful.

Flying low over a deep trench, his shadow sent a field mouse scurrying for cover. Along a field that sloped steeply to meet the sandy banks of the river he quartered diligently. Flying through a quiet breeze, his face to the river, he watched a dipper sitting below the stone bridge. It seemed agitated by his presence, bobbing up and down on a rock, then took itself away, flying fast and low over the river. Grey wagtails combed for insects on the granite wall of the bridge, then flew for cover when he got near.

Alighting on the hazels near the river, Vega sat bolt upright on an outer branch and looked around. The eastern skies were bright with watery reflections. Billowing clouds poured slowly by. He watched the black-headed gulls trail across the sky. Rousing himself, he decided to bathe at the water's edge. The shallow gravelly spot was ideal for bathing. He glided down and immersed his body feathers in cool water, then eased himself lower so that the water could reach his back feathers. It felt good. He began a playful mock attack on floating leaves drifting on the surface.

After splashing for quite some time Vega became aware of someone watching him. It was Sheila the heron. Her cold stare made him nervous as she held her motionless stance.

'I didn't know you kestrels were such water lovers.'

Vega said nothing but began to shake himself dry.

'You're new around these parts,' she continued, eyeing him closely.

'Oh yes ... I escaped from the falconry.'

'Really!' said a surprised heron. 'I know most of the birds there. Sad to hear about Capella the eagle. He was a dear friend.'

'He was a good friend of mine too,' replied Vega.

'Indeed,' said Sheila. 'Well, be careful. Get yourself up on that alder tree and dry yourself off. There are mink, stoats and stray cats around here who would

like to make a meal of a waterlogged falcon, so be off with you.'

Vega found it difficult to lift off but with tentative flight he glided to a perch on the alder, then sat with wings outstretched, and rested.

Post-bathing drowsiness set in and he began to doze, sitting quietly for a long time, allowing the warm day and gentle breeze to dry his feathers. He was conscious of the heron as she stood hunched over the water on her long stilts of legs; with targeting eyes she scanned the river for her next meal of fish or frog.

Then, suddenly, there was a loud clatter of wings as a wood pigeon lifted in a hurry from a beech tree. This startled Vega. Behind him the heron flapped into the sky. There was a flash of brilliant blue and emerald green as a kingfisher sped upriver. The kestrel looked around to see what had disturbed them all.

A Nusham was strolling up the ploughed field.

Vega sat tight. He knew that the Nusham did not see him. The Nusham held the death gun in one hand.

On his shoulder he carried a green bag. Suddenly he stopped, laid the gun down on the grass and took a dead rabbit from the bag. Cutting it with a knife he trailed the bloody body along the ground, then walked over to a small copse and threw the rabbit a few yards from the trees. The Nusham crouched quietly, shotgun held tightly with both hands.

Vega had been told about the death gun by Capella, and he had heard its terrible sound. Many times the silence of the falconry had been shattered by the blast of the death gun ending the life of some wild creature.

Time passed slowly. Vega caught sight of a fox in the distance. It moved warily and seemed to be trailing something; its nose searched the air.

The fox circled nervously, smelling the warm rabbit carcass, but there was also the heavy smell of Nusham. He continued to make his way down the field, stopping occasionally to sniff the air. Vega called loudly in alarm. The fox froze momentarily, then continued on, slipping under a fence. The smell of rabbit was strong.

The Nusham steadied and levelled his gun while the fox padded over and found the corpse. It was a freshly killed rabbit. Vega screamed louder, but to no avail. The muzzle of the gun was pushed through the thicket. Suddenly there was a loud shotgun blast. The fox was thrown clear off the ground, then he fell, writhing in agony, blood oozing from his side. He tried to stand but his legs buckled and he collapsed, body heaving, legs kicking. Stinging with pain, he rolled and twisted. Then he lay in a heap, jerking with the spasms of the dying. His fur was blood-stained and blood ran from his nose. He became still.

Bluebottles settled quickly on the dead fox, moving over the warm blood. The Nusham approached, kicked at the lifeless corpse, then walked slowly away, gun resting on his shoulder.

A male pheasant, feeding in a field of barley, was shot later that day.

*　　*　　*

A ribbon of pink stretched across the sky as the dusk, bringing its silence, closed in. Something stirred below, the shift and scurry of a field mouse. Vega's eye fastened upon it, then swooping down he raked the mouse with sharp talons. He mantled his kill, then gulped it down. Vega had finally caught a substantial meal. He knew he had to kill to eat, but why did the Nusham have to kill the fox? It was not to eat, so why? he wondered. The smoke gun had brought him a new dimension of fear, which he would never forget.

Across the evening shadows rooks called noisily as they returned from the fields. They would settle on the topmost branches of the beech trees that lined the hills. Vega flew to a post, watching the darkness move in over the fields. In the distance an owl screeched, then a rustle among the thistles revealed a hedgehog. It trundled nearer, turned over a cowpat and quickly gobbled up the beetles hiding on the underside.

'Hotchiwichi!' the kestrel called.

The hedgehog immediately rolled up into a ball, then uncurled himself after a few moments.

'Anyone who knows my name must be a friend,' he declared.

Vega flew down to him. Both of them were surprised and delighted to meet up again.

'Thank you for setting me free, Hotchiwichi,' said Vega.

'Well, Capella would be proud of you,' said the old hedgehog. 'Able to fend for yourself!'

'Only just,' retorted Vega.

'Your life has been blessed,' the hedgehog mused. 'You couldn't have had a finer teacher than Capella.'

'It's strange how a chance encounter can transform one's life,' said Vega. 'Capella never let up, and now I've discovered what it really means to be free!'

'A true mentor and friend,' observed Hotchiwichi. 'Well, remember young friend, the lessons of wisdom are useful only if they're understood and shared.'

Something moved behind them. The kestrel swivelled his head. He could see a fox standing in the shadows; it had crept up on them. Vega trembled and gaped at the fox, who padded out from the undergrowth.

'Sorry if I startled you.' The fox spoke gently and his eyes were soft and friendly.

'Hello, Crag,' said the hedgehog. 'This is Vega – an escapee from the falconry.' Then he added proudly, 'A friend of Capella.'

'You're welcome here,' said Crag. 'I know all about

the falconry. Young Kos, the barn owl, was a prisoner there for a time.' Vega remembered seeing the barn owl one night.

'Come and join us,' Crag continued. 'There's an important meeting taking place near the old quarry, which concerns all of us. You're not too tired?'

'Oh no,' said Vega. 'Lead on.'

The kestrel let the fox and the hedgehog move on ahead, then he would fly to them. He watched as they padded slowly up the field, stopping abruptly when they came close to the body of the fox. Crag circled it cautiously, sniffing the air nervously. He stared, alert, ears twitching, straining for any sound. All seemed quiet and safe. Vega swung into the air, flapped, then alighted on a fence post close by. Crag looked sadly on the broken form, tears in his eyes ready to spill over.

'It's old Towler from Clane. He's been a traveller ever since his she-fox and cubs were killed by the dogs. His fondness for pheasant was his downfall. Crag gave three howls over the body as a mark of respect to his old companion.

'I heard the gunfire earlier,' said Hotchiwichi. 'I knew it sounded the death-knell for some unfortunate wildfolk.'

'If it's not the dogs, the hedge wire or the gin traps, then it's the gun,' sighed the fox.

They continued on, their movements unhurried. As they passed the lake a frog plopped into the water. The wind rustled through the reeds. Crag sniffed as if decoding the wind. Vega watched, feathers puffed out to keep warm.

'Not too far now,' said the old fox. Suddenly he stopped, for up ahead were two mute swans, a cygnet and a moorhen, all lying dead by the lake. White feathers from the swans were strewn about. Crag's eyes darkened. What's happened here? he wondered.

The delicately beautiful form of the pen now looked grotesque in its twisted frozen state. There were small bites all along the neck of the cob. Their primary feathers were broken. Crag could get a strong smell of rat, and saw the small footprints in the muck.

The hedgehog found a black rat lying dead. 'How curious! A city rat out here.'

'We'd better report this to the Council,' said Crag, fearing the worst. They moved on, like shadows in late evening, past an outcrop of trees. The moon floated in the starlit sky as a light breeze carried the cold of darkness.

Barkwood, the long-eared owl, skimmed over them.

'Night peace to you, friends. I'll tell the others that you're on your way.' He slipped away silently through the night shadows that slid across the woods. Up ahead stood stark silhouettes of large boulders.

'We're nearly there,' said Crag, nosing the air, ears erect; he primed them for any sound.

The Council members watched the loping gait of Crag as he moved over some rocks into the clearing.

'Night peace to you all,' greeted Crag.

Barkwood the long-eared owl, Sheila the heron, Lutra the otter, and Hob the stoat were present, as were a party of grey squirrels from Celbridge and red squirrels from Donadea.

'You all know Hotchiwichi,' said Crag.

The hedgehog moved to the centre. Vega alighted beside Barkwood on a tall boulder.

'This is Vega. He was a good friend of old Capella, the eagle from the falconry.'

'We've met,' said Sheila. 'He made a big splash with me earlier.'

Hara and Sara, the hares, arrived, both with gashes on their backs. They explained how they'd been attacked by a band of black rats near the old mill. They'd managed to shake them off and outrun them but it was very frightening, related Sara.

Then six buck rabbits told the Council of the massacre at the ancient site, when the warren was ambushed by marauding cats and huge rats with stars on their fur, and how old Cuniculus was mortally wounded.

The Council listened with mounting horror and revulsion as the rabbits related their tragic tale.

'Sorry I'm late,' boomed a voice. Bawson the badger trundled in and, trembling all over, began to tell them how he had been out foraging in the barley fields near Clane and found over fifty pheasants lying dead, their heads bitten off.

'At first I thought it was the Nusham and the smoke guns, then wondered perhaps was it dogs, but on closer inspection I discovered it was rats ... thousands of them. I saw them, moving over the fields like a sea of fur, squealing, scurrying, writhing and twisting. I lay hidden in the hedgerow. Buck rats, doe rats, sow rats, scaldies, mangy, half crippled – all there. But what was even more worrying was the fact that cats were running with them – over fifty of them. Crag will tell you I have had dreams about this happening.

'Nightmares!' remarked Crag.

'Yes,' said Bawson. 'Nightmares. And now they've come true. Just like before with the last rat invasion.

'Only this time they've joined forces with marauding cats,' added Crag. 'How did they manage that, I wonder?'

Kos and Crannóg glided in over the boulders and landed on the ground beside Hotchiwichi. They reported hordes of rats on the move towards the ancient burial site.

'Ratland!' cried Crag. 'That's where they're heading.'

'Who cares if they go to Ratland?' said Sheila. 'What I'd like to know is why all the destruction along the way?'

Sara the hare, licking her wounds, replied: 'Probably to get the Nusham so mad that they'll kill every fox, badger, stoat, otter and any other wild creature they can find to blame. They'll set more dogs on us.'

'There will be more traps, poison and guns if we don't do something,' said Lutra the otter.

'I'm expecting Shimmer the rook to arrive at first light. Maybe we should rest till then,' said Crag.

Kos, Crannóg and Barkwood decided to scout the area for any information that might be useful.

Crag sat keeping guard while his friends slept.

CHAPTER 14

Caught in the Act

A reluctant sun rose over the sky, illuminating fields that glistened with dew. From the uppermost branches of a beech tree, now completely denuded of its leaves, Shimmer roused himself, preened a little and lifted into the air, flapping and gliding over the silent fields. Rooks with sleepy eyes watched their leader flap quietly away.

Meanwhile Kos was silently quartering the ground in slow flight, hovering for a while, then moving off. Gliding over the upper meadow, he spotted a huge rat which had a star on its back. He swooped down and grabbed it with his sharp talons. However, he decided not to kill it, but to bring it back to the Council. The rat, wild-eyed, twisted and turned, trying to set itself free. It bit at the owl's legs, but Kos held on and flew back quickly to the quarry. Shimmer was there talking to the others. When Crannóg saw Kos with the wriggling rat she hurried to assist. They both pinned it down. The others moved closer and circled the rat.

'What does the star on your back mean?' asked Sheila the heron.

'What's the meaning of all the slaughter?' demanded Bawson the badger.

'Where have you come from?' asked Hob the stoat. 'And how is it that there are city rats in our fields?'

'You'll get no answers out of me,' hissed the star rat. 'But I can tell you that Prince Natas will destroy every one of you.'

'I've a good mind to run you through,' threatened Sheila, holding her head back, ready to strike.

Barkwood arrived, carrying a rat in his beak. He alighted beside the barn owls, transferring the rat to his sharp talons.

'This one has the smell of the city on him,' said Barkwood.

Crag nosed him and said firmly: 'Don't I know you? You are the one called "Spike".'

The rat trembled. 'Please don't kill me. I was forced to come here.'

'Keep quiet,' yelled the star rat, 'or I'll tear out your throat.'

'You are in no position to make threats,' snapped Lutra.

'If you value your hide you'll tell us all,' Crag threatened.

Spike looked nervously at the star rat, then explained how Prince Natas had arrived from foreign parts with the star rats and that their aim was to continue the work of the Emperor Fericul, to re-establish Ratland and kill all their enemies.

'His words, not mine,' added Spike.

The star rat gave an evil grin. 'Now that we've discovered our ancient home we've only one more place to invade and then we'll be all-powerful and rule supreme!'

Shimmer shuddered for he knew there was only one place where they could reign supreme and that was the Sacred Cliffs. The Council members looked at each other in horror, knowing that if the rats tapped into the power of the Sacred Cliffs then no other creatures would be safe.

'We've heard of the all-powerful Sacred Feather. We shall unleash its energy!' the star rat grinned.

'What will we do with these rats?' asked Sheila, after some moments of stunned silence.

'Let them go,' said Crag. Then he spoke threateningly to the rats: 'Tell your Prince Natas we'll protect the Sacred Cliffs at all costs. If he or his kind try to desecrate the Cliffs he'll bring down destruction upon himself and all others who are in league with him.'

* * *

'I'll fly ahead to warn the Council of Ravens,' said Shimmer. 'The rest of you had better travel under the cloak of night.'

'Can I go with you?' asked Vega.

'No, my friend!' replied Shimmer. 'It's too dangerous. But maybe you could find more help for us.'

'Take care,' said Kos, as Shimmer flapped quickly into the sky, and away over the treetops.

'Go!' Crag commanded the star rat. 'Tell your leader we mean business, and that we'll fight him tooth and claw if he tries to invade the Sacred Cliffs.'

The owls loosened their grip on the star rat, who swung around quickly and bit deeply into Crannóg, then bolted through the rocks to the undergrowth.

Vega darted after the rat and found it scurrying through the long grass. He swung at it with his feet and pierced it through the back, killing it instantly.

Crannóg's leg throbbed with pain as red blood oozed through her feathers. Vega flew back and dropped the lifeless rat on the ground.

'Good work,' said Hob.

Vega trembled with relief. Crag glared at Spike.

'Go tell your leader what we said.'

The rat moved away slowly until he passed the rocks, then with great haste he headed for Ratland.

'At star light we'll meet,' said Crag

Kos suggested to Crannóg that she should return to the castle and rest. She flapped silently away, having entreated them all to take care.

Sheila decided to get something to eat, as she didn't like to fight on an empty stomach.

They all departed to meet again at evening glow.

'Well, my young friend, you've proved yourself to the Council tonight. They were very impressed,' said Hotchiwichi to Vega. Then he yawned loudly: 'I'm going for a nap. You should rest up too.' Crawling under a boulder, the hedgehog fell sound asleep.

The kestrel watched the others move away into the distance. Shimmer's words, 'Maybe you can find some help for us', circled his mind. But where could he find help? he wondered. There were lots of friends in the falconry but they were all prisoners, and there was no way he could release them. The only wild friends he knew were already prepared to do battle against Prince Natas. If only Capella were here, he would know how to advise.

That was it! Capella's clan, who lived at Mount Eagle! They would surely help. But where to find them; that was the problem. The only solution was to fly back to the falconry. One of the birds there would surely know – perhaps the black vulture, since he was Capella's oldest friend. The thought of the falconry made him shudder. What if he were caught and tied again to a block. He had just gained his freedom; he certainly wasn't about to give it up.

Vega had never heard of the Sacred Cliffs, yet his new friends were prepared to risk life itself to defend the place. Then he thought of Hotchiwichi's bravery towards himself. The old hedgehog had run the risk of a dog attack just to free him! There was nothing for it but to take the risk and go back to the falconry.

Arching his wings Vega slipped away over the quarry. A blackbird called in alarm from a hazel tree. Barkwood, from a larch, watched the young kestrel winging his way in the full light of morning.

As Vega approached the falconry his heart began to pound. He alighted on a hollow beech tree, but became completely unnerved by the sounds of a red squirrel, leaving its drey to search for nuts. Vega flapped away and flew to a laurel tree. From there he could see the birds sitting on their blocks as always, some preening, others just sitting still. Wagtails and finches were busy feeding around the falconry.

The kestrel flew over and landed on a hut near the black vulture. The birds couldn't believe it. Here was the young kestrel, returned. It's Vega! His name resounded round the falconry.

'What's Vega doing back here? Is he mad?' cried the cara cara.

The black vulture had been napping. His eyes widened with disbelief.

'Vega, it's good to see you, but what are you doing here? It's not safe. If the Nusham comes out he'll surely try to catch you.' The other birds crouched and stared, eager to know why the kestrel should return in broad daylight.

'I need your help,' said Vega. 'I must find out where Capella's clan lives.'

'Well, that's a difficult one,' said the black vulture as he ruffled his large wings. 'You have to fly north to the highlands, but it means crossing the sea. It's a long, dangerous journey for someone like you, not long on the wing. Indeed for any kestrel it would be difficult,' he said seriously.

'I must go,' said Vega. 'The Sacred Cliffs are in danger of invasion by rats.'

'Rats ...' pondered the cara cara, who was listening intently. 'Strange. Only two days ago a band of rats raided the falconry and hurried away with all the dead day-old chicks that are kept in the shed for us. The Nusham blasted some of them with a shotgun. More had climbed into the other sheds for cover but they were finished off by the snowy owls and the barred owls.'

'A rat named Natas has landed on our shores and has persuaded all the rats, and even city cats, to attack the Sacred Cliffs,' said Vega. 'The Cliffs are home to the Council of Ravens, where a Sacred Feather is held, said to be from the Eagle of Light.'

'This is very serious,' said the black vulture. He offered Vega some food that was left over. 'It'll keep hunger at bay. You'll need all your strength for the journey.'

The kestrel accepted the kind offer of the food and tore at the beef. It tasted sweet. When he had a full crop, he decided to leave. They all wished him well and he arrowed through the air on pointed wings, out over the treetops. The Nusham happened to be watching from the window as the kestrel gained height in the sky. He realised this was his kestrel, the same kestrel that had escaped from the falconry. There was no mistaking it, for the jesses were still on its legs. He hurried out the door but the bird was long gone. Annoyance gave way to admiration while he watched the kestrel making its winding ascent into the sky.

The other birds cheered and flapped with excitement as Vega circled in the crisp morning air.

The black vulture remained sitting quietly on his block. He remembered Capella, who was blessed with sublime wisdom, saying: 'Life is the real teacher; it offers many experiences. Some experience many things but learn little.' The black vulture sensed that Vega was learning fast. He felt very proud of him.

*　　*　　*

Vega shook his wings in mid-flight as if to discard any oppressive aura that might cling to him from the falconry. He sensed somehow that he was unravelling life's mystery. In a short span of time he had tasted joy, friendship, doubt, fear, and even terror.

Now, as he swung in the air above the falconry, the sky was filled with ominous clouds. Things became unnaturally still. He felt burdened by the obligation to get help and wasn't even sure if he could fulfil it. A strong breeze blew as if impelling him forward.

CHAPTER 15

Dark Deeds

The sky darkened and distant rumbling thunder could be heard as Spike arrived back at the ancient burial site. A solitary crow called from the dead trees. Up ahead the tall standing stones stood silent as the grave. Spike glanced at the mysterious carving – a legacy of some remote age. He quickly hurried past, on into the secret chambers, over the dry bones of Nusham, along the damp corridors until he reached the passage of skulls. Down he descended, nervously. Darkness closed behind him.

Natas's voice echoed through the chambers. 'I am the Master of Darkness and you are my servants. I will influence and guide you all!'

A mighty feast was in progress. Thunderous screeches and wails from the rodents pierced the chambers as they applauded the Prince.

Hack eyed Spike as he re-entered the bowels of Ratland. Spike shivered and shook. Spook whispered to Natas that Spike had arrived.

'Silence,' demanded the Prince. 'Our servant Spike has returned with good news, I hope.' He licked his black bristling fur.

All eyes watched Spike as he moved into the centre of the chamber, snout twitching and legs trembling. He squatted on his haunches. 'Greetings, Noble Prince of Eternal Night, hero of all creatures and guardian of–'

'Enough flattery!' interrupted Natas. 'I see you're on your own.'

Spike trembled. 'Well, I have good news and bad news.'

Natas stared hard at Spike. The whole chamber was silent. The silence became more frightening than sound. The rats, squatting, wriggling and squirming, had all eyes and snouts fixed on him.

'Well, Your Highness, we did according to Spook's plan, with your regal consent, of course. We went to the feral cats. They captured several street pigeons. They ate most of them, but saved three for the plan. It was very difficult but we managed to find some toxic poison stored near the dump. We bathed the pigeons as Spook suggested in the vile-smelling poison. One of them died because he swallowed some. The other pigeons were placed in a small cardboard box where the liquid poison dried into their feathers.

'Six cats came with us, each taking a turn to carry the box. We had to put wire through the box and get a cat to carry it on its back.'

'All very interesting,' said Natas, annoyed. 'But what happened?'

'Well, as Hack and I said, it was impossible to reach the Sacred Cliffs without passing the peregrines. As you know it was they who killed the great leader Fericul and our friend Thrasher.'

Spike could see the Prince was becoming more angry, so he quickly added that they released the pigeons into the air near the Cliffs and described how the pigeons flew on panicked wings for cover.

'The hungry peregrines eyed them with a predatory gleam, climbing to a great height in the raw wind. The pigeons tried to escape by flying out to sea, but down from their great height came the tiercel and peregrine, dive-bombing the pigeons, snatching them from the sky.

'They flew to a plucking post. We watched them from the granite rocks, plucking beakfuls of feathers before making a meal of the pigeons. Nothing happened for ages as they ate through the pigeon breasts, then they began to gape.

'Their bodies heaved and jerked; they rolled and twisted in agony, then came down in a flop. When we got to them they were as dead as the stones.'

There was an outburst of resounding cheers around the chambers.

Then quickly Spike added, 'As we journeyed back to Ratland we were savagely attacked by our enemies, the very ones that had invaded Ratland during the reign of Emperor Fericul. We fought bravely, the star rat and I, but we were heavily outnumbered and the star rat was killed.

'I managed to escape but not before I found out their plan to go to the Sacred Cliffs and join forces with the ravens to prevent us from claiming the Sacred Feather for ourselves.'

Natas did not seem too concerned that a member of his private army was killed, but he was angry that he had to push forward his plans for the invasion. 'When are our enemies going to the Sacred Cliffs?'

'They meet at dusk, as it will be safer to travel then,' replied Spike.

'We must leave now,' said Prince Natas. 'We must risk all for the glory of Rodents!'

All the rats repeated loudly: 'We must risk all for the glory of Rodents!'

'Away my friends,' cried Natas. 'Follow Hack and Spike. They'll lead the way to victory!'

The rats poured out of the chambers and up through the tunnels to the exit. Outside, the rain pelted down as they rushed headlong down the hill, hell bent on doing the Prince's will.

Before Natas left he spoke to Spook. 'You might be able to do your ghost trick with the ravens.'

'With all due respect,' replied Spook, 'ravens are far more clever than rabbits.'

'So, what do you suggest?'

'Well, we could pretend I contracted some terrible disease because of the Nusham, and that it's spreading throughout the animal kingdom. Some die instantly like the peregrine guards, others turn white and die slowly.'

'Brilliant!' said Natas. 'You *are* clever, dear Spook.'

'When we get the Sacred Feather you will have total power,' added Spook.

'Yes!' said Natas, nose flaring. 'But I'll not be using its magic to give rats the power of flight. I'll use it to destroy my enemies. I'll also wipe out the cats when I no longer have need of them. But not a word of this to anyone. Understand!'

Spook nodded reverently, then they left.

*　　*　　*

The sky began to clear after the heavy downpour. Slanting rays from the setting sun broke over the sea. The ravens sat on the plateau, eyes fastened on the white rat. Granet, one of their leaders, looked suspiciously at Spook; their eyes met straight on. Spook quivered as he began to spin his yarn of lies. The birds had a graven look, for they knew what the Nusham was capable of, and they were very upset by the mysterious death of the peregrines.

Corvus, one of the older ravens, whispered in Granet's ear. He reminded him that they had seen white creatures before and that there was no particular reason why this rat should be trusted. Below the plateau the hordes of rats and the feral cats waited, watching the ravens with Spook.

'What's happening?' hissed Natas. 'Hack, you and two star rats head over to assist Spook.'

They reluctantly scurried over. As they came closer the ravens swooped at them. 'How dare you enter this sacred place!'

'Please forgive us ...' cried Hack in a feeble voice, 'but we needed a refuge from our enemy, the

Nusham. They're destroying all the creatures in the valley below.'

The ravens examined the one-eyed Hack, and the other rats who had strange markings on their backs. They had never seen anything like them before.

'It's getting dark,' said Spook. 'If we can just rest for the night in your secret caves, then tomorrow we'll leave by first light.'

The ravens had a quick meeting among themselves.

'I don't trust them,' said Corvus.

Granet pondered. 'Well, in the Sacred Writings it is said, "We must help our fellow creatures when they call for help".'

Finally, Corvus gave his consent. He looked severely at the rats. 'Evening is closing in,' he said. 'Come and rest and have some food, but you must be gone by sunrise.'

*   *   *

Spook, Hack and the star rats slowly enter the mysterious caves. As they approach, a brilliant light shines from one of the inner passageways.

Hack exclaims loudly, 'The Sacred Feather!'

Granet stares at Hack. 'How do you know about the Sacred Feather?'

The ravens encircle the trembling rats. Dark menacing shadows loom large across the cave. The ravens turn in shock to discover cats and rats surrounding the entrance ...

CHAPTER 16

Bad Moon Rising

Darkness settled over the woods. Crag moved through them, sniffing the cold night air. He padded towards the fields which were laced with frost, and as he came out into the clearing, his friends were already beginning to gather. They came from all directions, silent, intent. There was a sense of foreboding among them. They knew they were facing a very dangerous mission. Bawson the badger, sniffing the air for scents, moved at a fresher pace to meet them. Barkwood and Kos arrived, weaving delicately over the trees.

Crag's eyes shone. 'Night peace, friends. We're all here except for Hotchiwichi.'

He eased himself onto his haunches. 'We're about to head off to the Sacred Cliffs. Our journey is a dangerous one. If anyone wants to remain, feel free to do so, and no one will think any the worse of you for your decision.'

The hares pondered among themselves and felt

they should remain behind as they had young to care for. Kos explained how Crannóg was still sleeping when he left the castle and he did not wish to disturb her. The rabbits felt they would be more of a hindrance than a help and so wished to remain in the lowlands. The squirrels felt the same. Bawson admitted that he didn't tell his cousins; they were still caring for young and he felt it would only worry them unduly.

From the woods they could hear the whispered chatter of the hedgehog as he hurried through the leaves.

'Sorry I'm late,' Hotchiwichi yawned. 'This weather makes me very sleepy.'

'Are you sure you're up to the journey?' asked Barkwood.

'Of course,' said Hotchiwichi. 'Fighting fit!'

'Well, we'd better go,' said Crag.

They slid away into the shadows, the other animals watching and wishing them well, as they moved along the fringe of the woods.

'I had a fearful dream ...' began Bawson.

'Not now, dear friend!' said Crag, as he loped lightly ahead.

Bawson lifted his head to the moon. It seemed to turn into a gleaming white skull. He quickly trundled up the field after the others. They moved in silence, passing under fences and along ditches until they reached a railway track that would lead to the Nusham city, and from there to the Sacred Cliffs.

Using the railway tunnels made the journey a little easier. It meant being safe from the prying eyes of Nusham or dogs. They moved in relative peace for a long time. Sheila the heron, Kos and Barkwood flew on to the railway station where they had agreed to meet the others. The plan was that they would all then journey together to the Cliffs.

The animals moved through the tunnel, making good progress. But after a time, peering through the

gloom, their eyes could discern a moving light. Crag glanced nervously as the yellow beam loomed larger through the darkness. They could now hear the whine of a machine.

'A train!' yelled Crag. 'Everyone off the track and keep very still!'

The animals had seen trains before but the beaming light and roaring noise made them tremble in terror. Its scream echoed through the night. The otter bobbed up and down then leapt over the track and stood beside the tunnel wall. The stoat followed. Bawson and Crag had taken to the other side. Hotchiwichi rolled into a ball in the sleepers. The train was gaining momentum as it lurched along the track.

Crag shouted at Hotchiwichi to come away from the track. His body was tucked in, close to the metal line. The fox leaped across to him and with his muzzle flicked him over the line. Then the hedgehog scurried behind Bawson. Closer and closer the train came, its light piercing the tunnel. The otter panicked and ran onto the track. The stoat scampered after him.

'No!' yelled Bawson, as the train screamed past, and hurtled along the track.

Crag, Bawson and Hotchiwichi moved cautiously out from the tunnel. The high-pitched screams of the otter and stoat had been muffled by the piercing roar of the train. Horror-stricken, the animals found the torn remains of their companions several yards up the track, their bodies sliced clean through by the grinding wheels. Their stomachs heaved at the sight of the shredded mass of red, bloody fur. They sat for some time in pained silence, then without a word moved on up the bank. Bawson knew now why he had seen the skull on the moon.

*   *   *

Kos circled above the station looking out for his friends. When they finally arrived he could see that there was something wrong. The birds flew down to greet them. With shaking voice Bawson related the sad news of the loss of their companions. There was a long silence.

'This mission is cursed,' said Sheila, breaking the silence. She declared that, in her opinion, they should abandon the idea of reaching the Sacred Cliffs and simply go home.

Crag said he would go on, his mind registering a

mental picture of what would happen should the rats get hold of the Sacred Feather. He knew it would be a nightmare for all other creatures if the rats were to triumph.

They took a vote. Kos, Barkwood, Bawson and Hotchiwichi agreed to journey on. Sheila said she would report the deaths to the otter and stoat clans, and, after wishing them success, she flapped away homewards on reluctant wings.

The wind blew cold as they moved purposefully through the city, past the towering shapes of buildings, in and out through pools of street lights. The streets were deserted now. Most of the Nusham were sleeping. The little group passed easily along by the canal but stopped in terror as they heard Nusham

voices up ahead. Two dishevelled figures sat on a bench, one with his head in his hands, the other drinking freely from a bottle. Grimy fingers reached out.

'Gimme a drop!'

The speaker clasped the sherry bottle tightly. The other Nusham jerked it back, roaring obscenities.

The animals held still, not daring to move. They were reluctant to pass the Nusham, but the only other way was to cross the water.

One of the Nusham looked over his shoulder and saw the animals framed against the street light. 'A fox and a badger ...' he muttered, rubbing his eyes.

It was decision time. Quickly the animals slipped past in the shadows.

'Do you know what I just saw?' the Nusham mumbled, grabbing the bottle again. He pointed at the ground. 'A fox and a badger ... right there.'

The other Nusham wiped his nose with the back of his hand, then wiped his hand on his coat. 'You're bloody daft!' he yelled and made a lunge for the bottle. He drank deeply.

The first one moaned. 'They were right there, I'm telling you ... as bold as brass ... just staring at me ...'

*　　*　　*

There was the smell of rain, and threatening clouds gathered. As the animals went for cover in a derelict building they felt the first spits of rain which soon became heavy, pelting down and forming large pud-

129

dles near the shore. They sat quietly listening as the rain pounded on the roof.

* * *

A light shifting mist moved over the cliffs. There was an unnatural quietness about. Kos and Barkwood circled up ahead. Crag and his companions were moving in on the ground. They were hoping Shimmer, the rook, would be there to greet them, but there was no sign of him. There was no sign of the peregrines either. This was most unusual; they always patrolled the Sacred Cliffs.

'There is a heavy smell of rats about,' said Crag. 'I don't like it.'

Then they saw a raven sitting near the entrance to a cave, preening the coverts of his great black wings. The owls flew over and alighted beside the raven. It

sat tight, not responding to their questioning. Crag, Bawson and Hotchiwichi joined them.

'We have come to warn the Council of Ravens of a possible attack by rodents,' said Barkwood. 'Has Shimmer the rook arrived?'

'Follow me,' said the raven, and he flew inside the cave.

'Keep watch out here, Hotchi,' said Crag. The fox nosed the air and followed the raven inside. Bawson, Kos and Barkwood entered. They could see Shimmer and the ravens ahead, but they didn't utter a word. As Crag moved closer a fishing net fell from the roof on to them.

'Got them,' cried Natas gleefully, as the rats poured out from their hiding places and pulled the net tightly. Crag snapped, Bawson clawed, but they couldn't tear the net. Spook and the star rats circled the net.

'What a catch!' said Prince Natas in mock laughter. 'So this is the army sent against me. I'm very disappointed.'

'I'm sorry I had to let you get caught,' said the raven who had led them into the cave, 'but if I didn't do as the rat commanded he would have killed all the Council members.'

Crag looked out through the net. He could see that Shimmer and the other ravens in the cave had their beaks tied with cord. By now the chamber was full of teeming, squealing rats. The floor was one black writhing mass of wriggling bodies, swarming over one another.

Spike and Hack whispered in the ear of the Prince that these were the enemies who had invaded Ratland and had been responsible for the demise of the Emperor Fericul. Natas turned a menacing eye towards them. His fur bristled, his scaly tail moved like a snake and his body emanated a malevolence that made Crag and his companions shudder.

Quietly the cats entered the cave. They all carried something in their mouths, then proudly dropped their kills of curlew, skylark, meadow pipit, ring ouzel, grouse and rabbit.

Natas shrieked with glee. 'Eat, drink and be merry, for tomorrow they die!'

Outside, Hotchiwichi the hedgehog circled the lichen-covered rocks in frenzied desperation, wondering how he could save his friends from those furry vermin.

CHAPTER 17

Mount Eagle

Vega moved over the swirling waves. He ached with tiredness. He had been battered all night by the torrential rain. Rising high in the sky, he watched the Manx shearwaters weaving over the waves. A gannet circled high, hovering over the water, then dropped like a stone into the sea, emerging seconds later with a fish in its dagger-shaped bill.

Flight-tired, the young kestrel continued wearily over the dark green sea. Now he could see land up ahead. The waves crashed against distant cliffs. As he moved closer the cliffs rose up. Passing over the sheer face that revealed the scars of ancient battles it had fought and lost with the sea, he alighted on a shelf that thrust out over the steep cliffs. The winds gusted against his body. A mixture of anticipation and dread accelerated his heart beat.

The sea ran wild below. Waves rose and crashed against the cliffs, then fell back to the water. Vega shivered. He felt overwhelmed by it all. Yet there was

a sense of satisfaction in having made the journey across the great dark sea. No matter how tired he was he found a great joy in flight. He watched the shags as they sat on the finger rocks above the swelling surf. They looked in his direction but took no notice of him.

Nearby a great black-backed gull hung in the air, then screamed down at him, mobbing him mercilessly. Vega ducked several times as the gull circled for a second attack. This proved too much for Vega. He was forced into the air to defend himself against the aggressor. The two birds jostled each other for some time in mid-air, stooping and screaming. Finally, the gull alighted on the exact spot where Vega had been resting, and called loudly in triumph.

Ahead the mountains rose in steep slopes. The winds off the mountains seemed to grace his wings with strength as he flew, wings which wind-hugged the air as he approached this mysterious place near the cloud-covered mountains. Ancient voices seemed to whisper on the wind as he glided through the mist.

Then his mind was assailed with terrible nagging fears. What if the eagles were gone? Or worse still, if they were there but hostile and tore him from the sky? He tried to shake off these thoughts.

Higher still he rose. The strong chilly winds gathered under his wings. He skimmed and floated lightly along a steep slope, eyes always wary for any movement. A ptarmigan sat crouched among rocks. Red

deer moved cautiously down the slopes. A stag, lifting up his head, looked over at Vega, then continued to pick its way along the rocks. The kestrel sailed, soared, flapped and glided over glens, peaks and corries, but there was no sign yet of Mount Eagle.

Finally Vega rested on a granite rock. He could see desolate snow-clad peaks ahead where the mountains grew sharper. Below were dark lochs, a cluster of hillocks and shattered rocks, now clearly visible through the clearing mist. Thoughts of the falconry floated into his mind. He thought of all those birds who wanted desperately to be free but who could only reach the sky through stories and memories.

Over the great northern ridges, covered with snow, a buzzard sailed and fanned the sky, hovering for a time, then moving on over some boulders. Vega watched as he circled overhead. The buzzard stopped and hovered briefly, then swooped down beside him.

Folding his big wings gracefully he spoke quietly to Vega. 'Are you lost? You're a little out of your range, you know. This is eagle country,' he added.

'Well, you're not an eagle either,' retorted the kestrel.

'True!' the buzzard agreed. 'But why are you up so high? You belong in the lowlands.'

'I have to find Mount Eagle,' said Vega.

'Why, that's on the next plateau. But they don't welcome strangers around here. Strangers usually mean trouble. Farewell!' And with a rush of wings he flapped away into a long glide over the slopes.

After a time Vega flew on towards the next peak. It was a long, upwind flight. It took him some time, swerving and twisting, soaring and gliding, until eventually he reached the plateau. All was still and quiet. He sat, endlessly scanning the landscape, but saw no sign of any eagles.

Yet this was the right place; this was Mount Eagle. He sensed that some mysterious force had guided him safely across the sky to the ancestral home of the eagles.

Suddenly his heart began to thunder in his chest, for he could see several eagles making their winding

descent from the sky, the birds' great wings casting massive shadows over the plateau.

'What are you doing here, little kestrel?' an eagle's voice boomed at him. Their large powerful wings brought them gently on to the ground. Vega gaped at their imposing presence. The wind stirred the eagles' feathers.

The older one stretched its yellow feet. 'Speak!' he said firmly, his voice charged with authority.

The other eagles remained very still, but stared coldly at Vega.

'He's got the mark of Nusham on him,' said one eagle sharply.

With that the old eagle noticed the leather jesses on the kestrel's legs. 'You have escaped from the Nusham!'

Vega wondered how he knew this.

'Well, you'd better clear off to the lowlands,' snapped another of the eagles.

'I come for help! I'm a friend of Capella, or rather was ...' All eyes were riveted on him now. The old eagle seemed in a daze. 'He died in a falconry,' Vega reflected sadly.

As the old eagle remembered Capella, the years came pouring back to him. 'My dear son, Capella. How he would dance through the air ...'

'It was he who had me set free; he taught me how to conquer the sky,' said Vega.

The old eagle let his head sink low. Vega stared at the massive beak. Suddenly the head lifted. 'What kind of help do you require?' he asked.

Vega looked into his sombre eyes and told him about the rat invasion. The old eagle gave a knowing look to the others, then turned to the kestrel.

'I'm called Sage. What do we call you?'

'Call me Vega,' said the kestrel proudly. 'Capella gave me that name.

The old eagle's eyes misted. 'You were truly a friend of Capella. Did you know that the night he was born Capella and Vega could be seen in the clear night sky!'

Then with a change of tone Sage commanded that two eagles hold the young kestrel down. Vega trembled as he lay on the soft grass. The old eagle moved his heavy beak slowly over him, then down to his legs. The kestrel closed his eyes. Carefully the eagle pecked the leather straps from his yellow legs and flicked them away.

'From now on, you'll have no mark of Nusham upon you. You are truly free.'

The eagles flapped their wings triumphantly. Vega sat up, ruffled his feathers and flapped his wings proudly.

'We'll rest awhile and eat. Later we'll decide what must be done,' declared Sage.

'But by then it might be too late!' cried Vega. 'They've gone to the Sacred Cliffs already ... they must be there by now. They might be in real danger. I must return at once.' He fluttered his wings, preparing them for flight.

'Farewell,' he yelled, as he soared across the sky.

The eagles watched Vega winging his way down the mountainside.

'What loyalty!' remarked Sage, as he watched the kestrel winging his way down the slopes.

Soon the young kestrel was out of sight.

Sage, the old eagle, stretched his wings. 'There may be great dangers awaiting him, even in the treacherous air currents.' He preened his old scraggy feathers. 'Maybe all this is preordained.'

'It would be good to help,' said another. 'But we haven't been to that island for such a long time. We don't know the dangers that might await us there. When our clan did fly those mountains they soon became extinct because of the death guns and the poison.'

'We're not totally free of those dangers here either,' remarked a female eagle.

'I think there should be a "Gathering of Eagles",' commanded Sage.

CHAPTER 18

War Lords

'Silence!' shouted Spook, 'Our Prince will now speak.'

Natas appeared from inside the cave. The bright light made him blink. He sniffed the air, then scratched his bristly fur. The rodents sat up, muzzles to the air in salute. The cats slunk out from the dark and circled the rodents. They sat on their haunches. The rodents tensed; they didn't feel secure with so many cats behind them. They whispered among themselves.

'Silence!' roared Natas.

They sat silently, not daring to move.

Then Natas took a deep breath and grinned. 'I'm just savouring the sweet smell of success.'

The rodents and cats hissed and shrieked loudly in adulation.

'My star rats and I promised you *everything*. Did we not keep our promise?'

More cheers and squeals from the crowd.

'We've won Ratland and now we've won the Sacred Cliffs. This is my domain. I've conquered all. Death or Glory!'

'Death or Glory!' the rodents yelled several times.

Then with a menacing stare Natas said quietly: 'I've been studying *The Sacred Book of Ravens* which has been kept hidden here. And on the first page that I opened do you know what it says?

> 'He who breaks a single link in the chain
> of love
> Breaks that chain ...'

He laughed a demonic laugh, the others forcing themselves into hysterical laughter. 'Silence,' Natas demanded. 'There is more.

> 'They who are against love
> Have the seed of the wicked.
> They shall be called the Spoilers.
> Beware of these Spoilers
> For they can invade and penetrate all
> creatures.'

The rodents were silent, but trembled at his words. He continued loudly:

> 'Where there is Violence
> There will you find the Spoilers.
>
> All has to be atoned for:
> The liar and the lie
> The murderer and the murdered.'

'Fine words indeed,' sneered Natas. 'But not very practical. For we know that power is might,' he hissed loudly. 'Violence and cruelty are the weapons of power, to be used by the strong to keep them powerful.'

With that he stretched out his arms. 'Bring out the enemies!'

Crag, Bawson, Kos, Barkwood, Shimmer and the Council of Ravens were all dragged out. The orange netting held them firmly.

'This sorry lot was sent against me, Natas the Mighty, Prince of the Underworld!' He pointed at them. 'This pathetic moth-eaten band dares to come against such a powerful army as mine. I find this insulting!' He flashed his yellow teeth. 'Let's see how well they swim.'

He gave them an icy gaze and ordered several rats to tie a large rock to the fish net. 'We shall roll them off their Sacred Cliffs and they too shall enjoy a watery grave, like our beloved Emperor Fericul.'

In their terrible excitement none noticed the hedgehog slipping out through a crack in the rocks, pulling the Sacred Feather with him. Moving farther over the boulders, Hotchiwichi kept whispering to the precious object, 'Please don't glow, please don't glow,' as the light expanded and retracted.

Suddenly a shadow was cast across Hotchiwichi. He trembled as he turned around slowly. There stood Vega, silhouetted against a pale sun.

'Oh heavens, it's you!' whispered the hedgehog.

'You gave me a most terrible fright.'

The kestrel jumped down beside him and explained how he had tried to get help from the eagles of Mount Eagle.

'You managed to fly all the way there?' asked the hedgehog.

'Oh yes – and back,' beamed the young kestrel.

* * *

Crag had spotted the hedgehog and when Hotchi-wichi was safely out of sight he yelled at Natas, 'Oh noble Prince, since we are about to die may we have one last request?'

The star rats moved quickly to silence the old fox.

'No! Comrades,' grinned Natas 'It's only fitting that we grant these prisoners a last request.'

Bawson looked blankly at Crag, wondering what on earth his friend would request.

'Well, Your Royal Highness, perhaps you could grant us a last look at the Sacred Feather.'

'Don't,' Hack whispered to Natas. 'It's some kind of trick.'

'I wouldn't trust that old fox,' added Spook.

'What could possibly happen by showing it to them?' asked Natas.

'I don't like it,' said Spike.

'Silence!' demanded Natas. 'Fetch the Sacred Feather.' Then he motioned to the star rats. 'All shall see my ultimate weapon.' He moved closer to the prisoners.

'Feast your eyes upon the Sacred Feather. It's the last thing you will ever see.' He turned towards the cave.

The star rats came out from the secret chambers. They were trembling.

'Where is the Feather?' demanded Natas, anger flowing through his body.

'It's gone!' mumbled a star rat.

'Gone! It can't be gone,' screamed Natas in a frenzied madness.

'The cats took it,' yelled Crag.

Then the rodents began to chant:

> 'The cats have stolen the Sacred Feather.
> The cats have stolen the Sacred Feather.'

There were screams and squeals of anger. Natas lunged at the leader of the cats.

'Where's my Feather, Moloch?'

The cat arched, lifted his paw, then revealed his claws.

'I haven't touched the Feather,' he spat back.

Turning slowly, Natas looked around with accusing eyes and fixed a stare on the cats, now crouched ready for battle. Natas exposed his teeth in a chilling grin, then moved in quiet aggression.

'We're all comrades here. Let's not fight over some Feather that's supposed to have magical powers. Let's be calm. It can't be too far away.'

The cats began to relax. Suddenly, in a high-pitched screech Natas yelled, 'Attack!'

Bodies arched. Fur bristled. Teeth flashed. The rodents leapt from the ground on to the cats.

'Kill them all! Death to the traitors!'

A running battle began between cats and rodents. Rats scrambled over cats' bodies, incisors sinking into backs, blood spurting through fur. Howls and screams came from the feral cats, who returned the attack, clenching jaws closing on live rats. Claws flayed the rodents, bodies crashed to the ground. The battle intensified. Teeth rammed straight into flesh, ripping writhing bodies. Limbs were torn clean off. Razor teeth slashed throats. Yelps, screams and squeals filled the air. Clawed feet tightened on cats' shoulders. Leaping, squirming, screeching, the rats continued their attack.

Suddenly all eyes were arrested by a beautiful light, and slowly the battle ceased. The light moved closer and closer. Natas, wide-eyed, watched Spook, Hack and Spike carrying the Sacred Feather.

'You've found it, my loyal comrades.'

They carefully laid it on the ground.

Crag, Bawson, Kos and Barkwood looked on in horror, for not only had the rats regained the Sacred Feather, but they had also captured Vega and Hotchiwichi.

'These are the ones who took it,' snapped Hack.

Vega and Hotchiwichi were held fast by several rats. Natas moved closer to them, full of rage.

'You've caused us great losses,' he muttered, looking at the bodies of dead rats and cats strewn about. 'Still, they can be replaced.' He turned to Moloch.

'Dear comrade, maybe I was too quick to accuse ... We've both suffered heavy losses, but we can rebuild our armies quickly, and as allies we shall be invincible. Nothing can stop us now ...'

But Natas stopped in mid-speech, because suddenly the skies darkened. The rats cowered and trembled as large black shadows were cast on the ground. Cats and rodents were transfixed by dark shapes circling out from the sun.

Cleaving the air, the eagles made their deadly descent. There were shrieks of disbelief as rodents and cats looked at the large dark forms. They tried to scramble and dart for cover, but it was too late. The eagles were upon them, swooping down and in for the kill. Natas snarled defiance at the eagles, standing at the cliff edge.

'Attack, Comrades, attack!' He roared at his army.

Old Sage dived and skimmed the rocks, with talons outstretched against the rats' leader. Steel grey talons struck home. Natas was dead in an instant.

Moloch leapt like a leopard into the air, hoping to bring down the big eagle. The eagle veered away, missing the cat's deadly attack. The cat fell back on to a rock. Another eagle made a vertical dive, swooped and knocked him clear off the rock into the raging sea. The battle was savage and bloody, but victory was assured because of the eagles.

*　　*　　*

The victors sat in the golden light of a westerly sun. A cool breeze blew in from the sea. The Council of Ravens thanked the eagles for protecting the Sacred Cliffs from their enemies.

'It's this young kestrel and his friends who are the true heroes,' said the old eagle.

'Well, it was your son, Capella, who inspired me!' Vega retorted. 'His love and faith gave me the courage to go on. I've learned to see through his eyes – with wisdom, compassion and a sense of wonder.'

The old eagle looked proudly at the young kestrel.

'We must all rest and feast,' suggested Granet, the raven.

They spent the evening sharing, listening and re-galing each other with stories. They sat around, bathed in the light of the Sacred Feather and felt comforted, healed and totally refreshed.

*   *   *

In the chill of the night Spook, Hack and Spike came out of hiding, tense and quivering. Moving cautiously, they scuttled away down the hills, not stopping until they reached the security of the city dump. There were many furry rodents to greet them. They were sombre as the three told them what had happened. Spook looked out at the night, then whispered to Hack and Spike, 'Natas said he would send a wave of extinction to all who defied him. All he succeeded in doing was to make himself extinct.'

Hack laughed nervously.

'Let's eat,' said Spike. 'I'm starving.'

They slid underground to their safe chambers, where they feasted and rested.

CHAPTER 19

All's Well that Ends Well

The sun kindled the sky with its fiery light. Night slipped away. Vega roused himself and preened. Shaking the drowsiness from his body he lifted off into the sky and hovered in the cold fresh morning air. Holding his body at an angle to the wind he fanned out his tail. With rapid wingbeats he remained in one spot, his sharp eyes scanning the vegetation for the slightest movement. Nothing was stirring so he glided away and took up a new position. It felt so good, it was as if he had blended into the sky. Only on the wind did he become truly alive. He reflected on Sage, the golden eagle, and his parting words as they took off for Mount Eagle:

'May the years smile upon you
May your wings always beat free.'

As he hung in the air he knew that he was born for the sky. He thought of all his friends: Hotchiwichi who was now in deep hibernation under some leaves, Kos whom he loved to see quartering the fields at dusk, Crag, Bawson and Shimmer – they were friends for life.

Vega felt relaxed and at peace with life in the drifting silence. Gently he shifted into a different part of the field. Suddenly he saw Kos, flapping fast and furious over the river, followed by Shimmer. He wondered why they were in such a hurry. Only something serious would bring the barn owl out in daylight ...

They circled Vega.

'What's up?' he enquired, tensing his body.

'No time to explain,' said Kos. 'Follow us. Now!'

The barn owl and the rook flapped towards the woods. Vega searched the sky for any danger, trying to fathom the mystery, then sped after them. As they reached the edge of the woods Crag, Bawson, Cran-nóg and Barkwood sat anxiously waiting. Crag seemed unusually nervous and paced up and down. When Kos and Shimmer alighted on the fence Vega quickly swooped in and sat on a post. His head bobbed anxiously.

'What's happening?'

'Shush!' said Crag.

Then from a horse chestnut tree two falcons glided gracefully over and alighted next to Vega. The young kestrel looked puzzled as he stared at the handsome male and female. They gazed at one other in silence for a long time.

'Well, have you nothing to say to your parents?' asked Crag.

Vega was speechless. All three were overwhelmed with joy. They preened one another affectionately and nuzzled one another's necks in welcome.

Bawson explained how a member of Shimmer's rookery had witnessed the destruction of the beech tree and had watched the Nusham collect one of the eggs and bring it to the falconry.

'So, you see, you always had wild wings.'

Vega's parents, Falco and Cymbeline, thanked the others for re-uniting them with their only offspring.

'I've experienced many things, and seen many amazing signs, but what I've learned to treasure most is friendship,' said a grateful Vega.

'Away!' said Barkwood. 'Let your wings whisper your secrets to the wind.'

Then, with upraised wings the young kestrel and his parents swung into the air, soared and fanned into the welcoming sky.

Bawson said to Crag, 'Did I tell you about the dream I had the other night?'

'I hope I wasn't in it,' replied the old fox, as he scratched behind his ear.

Other books from
THE O'BRIEN PRESS

From DON CONROY

The WINGS series

ON SILENT WINGS

A young owl, Kos, is left alone when its mother dies in a trap. He must learn to survive in a world full of danger and threatened by King Rat and his followers.

Paperback £4.99

SKY WINGS

The Feather of Light at the Sacred Cliffs protects the world from darkness. A young falcon, Sacer, must try to take it to Ratland in an attempt to wipe out the forces of evil.

Paperback £4.50

THE CELESTIAL CHILD

A boy who can speak to animals, take away pain, and eliminate pollution arrives from nowhere. What can Sarah and her friends learn from him?

Paperback £3.99

The WOODLAND FRIENDS series

THE OWL WHO COULDN'T GIVE A HOOT!

An owl who cannot hoot? The woodland friends try to solve this strange mystery ...

THE TIGER WHO WAS A ROARING SUCCESS!

An visitor from foreign lands arrives in the woodlands, but can the friends help him return home again?

THE HEDGEHOG'S PRICKLY PROBLEM!

Harry Hedgehog joins the circus – and gets into some sticky situations ...

THE BAT WHO WAS ALL IN A FLAP!

Ever hear of a flying fox? Harry Hedgehog *sees* one, and throws everyone into confusion ...

All Paperback £3.99

Learn to DRAW ...

CARTOON FUN

Learn to draw cartoons from a master. Great fun and really successful.

Paperback £4.95

WILDLIFE FUN

Learn to draw wildlife, in realistic and cartoon form.

Paperback £4.99

* * *

AMELIA
Siobhán Parkinson

Almost thirteen, Amelia Pim, daughter of a wealthy Dublin Quaker family, loves frocks and parties – but now she must learn to live with poverty and the disgrace of a mother arrested for suffragette activities.

Paperback £3.99

THE CHIEFTAIN'S DAUGHTER
Sam McBratney

A boy fostered with a remote Irish tribe 1500 years ago becomes involved in a local feud and with the fate of his beloved Frann, the Chieftain's daughter.

Paperback £3.99

THE BLUE HORSE
Marita Conlon-McKenna

When their caravan burns down, Katie's family must move to a house on a new estate. But for Katie, this means trouble.

Paperback £3.99

NO GOODBYE
Marita Conlon-McKenna

When their mother leaves, the four children and their father must learn to cope without her. It is a trial separation between their parents. Gradually, they all come to deal with it in their own way.

Paperback £3.99

THE HUNTER'S MOON
Orla Melling

Cousins Findabhair and Gwen defy an ancient law at Tara, and Findabhair is abducted. In a sequence of amazing happenings, Gwen tries to retrieve her cousin from the Otherworld.

Paperback £3.99

THE SINGING STONE
Orla Melling

A gift of ancient books sparks off a visit to Ireland by a young girl. Her destiny becomes clear – *she* has been chosen to recover the four treasures of the Tuatha de Danann. All her ingenuity and courage are needed.

Paperback £3.99

THE DRUID'S TUNE
Orla Melling

Two teenage visitors to Ireland are hurled into the ancient past and become involved in the wild and heroic life of Cuchulainn and in the fierce battle of the Táin.

Paperback £4.50

MISSING SISTERS
Gregory Maguire

In a fire in a holiday home, Alice's favourite nun is injured and disappears to hospital. Back at the orphanage, Alice is faced with difficult choices, then a surprise enters her life when she meets a girl called Miami.

Paperback £3.99

CHEROKEE
Creina Mansfield

Gene's grandfather Cherokee is a famous jazz musician and Gene travels the world with him. He loves the life and his only ambition is to be a musician too. But his aunt has other plans!

Paperback £3.99

COULD THIS BE LOVE? I WONDERED
Marilyn Taylor

First love for Jackie is full of anxiety, hope, discovery. Kev *seems* to be interested in her, but is he really? Why is he withdrawn? And what can she do about Sinead?

Paperback £3.99

UNDER THE HAWTHORN TREE
Marita Conlon-McKenna

Eily, Michael and Peggy are left without parents when the Great Famine strikes. They set out on a long and dangerous journey to find the great-aunts their mother told them about in her stories.

Paperback £3.99

WILDFLOWER GIRL
Marita Conlon-McKenna

Peggy, from *Under the Hawthorn Tree*, is now thirteen and must leave Ireland for America. What kind of life will she find there?

Hardback £6.95 Paperback £4.50

And many more, for adults and children.
Send for our full-colour catalogue.

THE O'BRIEN PRESS
20 Victoria Road, Dublin 6, Ireland
Tel: (01) 4923333 Fax: (01) 4922777